KICKI

'*Kicking Off* is a book about ⎯⎯⎯⎯⎯
Padgett is a skilful writer and ⎯⎯⎯⎯⎯
which he tackles place, memory ⎯⎯⎯ community
and above all change. It's a story of rising to the challenge
and camaraderie on and off the field'

IAN CLAYTON, WRITER AND BROADCASTER

'Mike Padgett shows impeccably that it isn't impossible for men to write strong and attractive female characters with depth and complexity...and he blends a cocktail of both the best and most frustrating tendencies in working class masculinity with warmth, subtlety and generosity'

*STEPHEN LINSTEAD, EMERITUS PROFESSOR,
YORK UNIVERSITY*

'Mike Padgett cleverly uses dialogue and character to wrestle with ideas and issues here'

IAN McMILLAN, POET

'A heart-warming and thought provoking story, celebrating second chances, challenging prejudices and showing that the biggest victories can happen off the pitch as well as on it'

*CAROL WEST, FORMER CHAIR OF THE
WOMEN'S NATIONAL LEAGUE*

'In *Kicking Off*, the basic story about the fight for women to play football, and to be accepted, is one that female footballers have battled for years. Passion, pride, and pleasure – that's football. Love it or not, (and we love it) it's definitely for everyone'

*MARRIE WIECZOREK, FORMER ENGLAND
AND MIDDLESBROUGH PLAYER AND
FORMER MIDDLESBROUGH MANAGER*

Also by Mike Padgett

AS FAR AS WE CAN

SCRAP

KICKING OFF

Mike Padgett

GRITSTONE
PUBLISHING

Published in 2025 by

Gritstone Publishing Co-operative Ltd.,
Birchcliffe Centre, Hebden Bridge HX7 8DG.

www.gritstonecoop.co.uk

© Mike Padgett 2025

ISBN 978-1-913625-16-0

The right of Mike Padgett to be identified as author of this work has
been asserted in accordance with the Copyright, Designs and Patents
Act 1988.

All rights reserved. No part of this publication may be reproduced,
stored in a retrieval system, or transmitted, in any form or by any
means, electronic, mechanical, photocopying, recording or otherwise,
without the prior permission of the publisher.

This book is a work of fiction. Any resemblance to people or events,
past or present, is purely coincidental.

1

The pint of lager in the beer garden behind the Miners Arms was the coolest and most refreshing Brian had ever drunk. He felt like pouring the last few inches down his back which was burning after a morning's overtime on a building site the other side of Wakefield. He shrugged the blue overalls off his shoulders, trying not to catch his red, prickly skin, and tied the sleeves around his bare waist. When he picked up his pint again the bald patch on top of his head began to burn. The sun was shining through a tear in the white parasol above his table. He shuffled along the wooden picnic bench to get out of the glare. A waiter carrying two plates of curry walked past shouting number thirteen, and Brian's favourite weekend fragrance hung in the air.

Across the road in Woodland Park the bandstand clock showed five to twelve. Brian checked his mobile. Half past one. The clock's gift of time added to his relaxed mood. He was five years old again, running through the park with the unleashed dogs; then ten years old, playing with the young kids on the swings; fifteen, hanging around the bandstand with his mates; twenty-one, playing football with the lads at the side of the bandstand.

'Spying on little kiddies in the park, Brian? They'll lock you up for that.'

Tommy Duggan and Spike, two old team mates from his footballing days, stood over him.

'I didn't think Clayton village was your stomping ground,' Brian said.

'We have no borders, do we Spike.'

'The highest razor wire fence in the whole of the land cannot imprison a determined man.'

Tommy Duggan and Spike stayed on their feet and laughed into each other's face. Brian remained seated, shook their hands and lied about how well they looked.

'I was watching what I thought were some young lads playing football. Looks like they might be a team of women. They're just coming out of the park, now.'

Duggan and Spike weren't listening. Their eyes were already scanning the beer garden. 'Any talent worth bothering with in here?' Duggan said. 'Save us going into Brodworth.'

A wasp landed on the rim of Brian's glass, antennae twitching, looking for a way down the slippery side, seemingly uninterested in a slightly overweight, five-foot ten body looming over it. He swore at the wasp and waved it away but it kept coming back.

'If I'd have been marking that little blighter when I was in my prime,' he said, 'I'd have soon sorted it out, sting or no sting.'

'I know you would,' Duggan said. 'You'd have flattened it. Whereas me, being a bit craftier, I'd have sneaked up behind it and taped its wings together.'

'Then you'd have annihilated it and fed it to the ants in your pants and the uncles in your carbuncles,' Spike said.

Brian swatted the wasp away and laughed at his old team mate. Spike inhabited a cryptic world. All of his friends and most of his doctors had given up trying to work out where he lived.

'Nothing changes, Spike,' Brian said. 'Where do you get them from?'

'The only place for change, me old cocker, is in the pocket.'

The eight women footballers Brian had been watching in the park tumbled out of the back door of the pub into the beer garden, laughing and pushing. Spike patted Brian on the head.

'I wouldn't mind being their physio for a week. Rubbing oils and water colours. Artist at work.'

Duggan spat into the palm of his hands and rubbed them together.

'You'd have to climb over me first.'

Brian closed his eyes and sighed. It was almost exactly the same conversation they had the last time they bumped into each other. That was twelve months ago in a pub in town one Saturday afternoon. The group of women being targeted on that occasion were on a spinster do, dressed in sexy underwear, and having a great time. Brian had laughed along with Duggan and Spike but then foolishly let the pair drag him around town on a pub crawl. He ended up being taken home in a wheelbarrow, apparently, and woke up next morning with a bloodied nose and a pink garter around his neck. That wasn't going to happen today.

Now the players looked over to Brian's table, their laughter evaporating as they tried to work out who had made the comments and why. One of the women wore a green tracksuit and carried a clipboard and pen. She was ten, maybe fifteen years older than the others and she stared the longest. Was that Jean from his dad's care home? It must be; not many women dyed their hair such a vivid red. Brian nodded. She nodded back, unsmiling.

'Who's that?' Duggan said.

'It's Jean. She works at the care home where my dad is.'

'Are you giving her one?' Spike said. 'Caring in the community?'

'Course he is,' Duggan said. 'Look at his face. Hey, are you coming into town with us again this aft?'

'We've booked a hand-propelled load-bearing vehicle especially for you,' Spike said, and Brian's two friends nearly choked on their beer.

The footballers, still in their training gear, socks around their ankles, grass stains down their shorts, found two tables a few yards from Brian's and began throwing the ball to each other. When one of them stretched up for a high ball, exposing her midriff, Spike nudged Duggan. Both put their pints up to their mouths without speaking and kept their eyes on the woman. Two players accidentally banged their heads together going for the same ball. There was a sharp intake of breath from everyone close by. Duggan and Spike laughed.

A little girl, eating fish and chips with her parents at the next picnic table, held out her arms and one of the players gently lobbed the ball to her. The little girl threw it back with all her strength, and the game soon spread to other tables. Duggan's face was red, his jaw set. The signs. Someone threw the ball to him and he fumbled it.

'You've still got it, Tommy,' Spike said.

'Piss off.'

People clapped a steady rhythm, waiting for the game to resume.

'Throw it to that half chat,' Spike said. 'Make her stretch her back like a big black cat.'

Duggan picked the ball up and, as if taking a long throw-in, launched it high over the heads of the women players into the car park at the other side of the fence. The beer garden went quiet.

'Stupid, noisy women,' Duggan said. 'Footballers? They should be at home getting the dinner ready.'

Customers picked up their knives and forks and quietly returned to what they were doing. One of the players jumped over the fence and slowly walked back with the ball.

'There was no need for that, Tommy,' Brian said. 'It was just a game.'

'Hey. Don't tell me what I can and can't do.'

There it was: the cold stare above the tight smile. Brian kept quiet. He pulled his overalls back over his shoulders and said he'd be two minutes. The players had stopped laughing now, and were listening to Jean review their training session. She paused when Brian came up to her table.

'I'm sorry about that, Jean. I think they've had a bit too much to drink.'

Jean stared past Brian, and spoke loud enough for Duggan and Spike to hear.

'We heard everything they said. It wasn't very nice.'

Duggan and Spike raised their pints and smiled to show Jean they could hear what she was saying and couldn't give a monkey's.

'They can be a bit macho at times,' Brian said. 'They think football's a man's game. We all played for the Acorn in the Sunday league many years ago. We won everything.'

'I wish my team had been around when you lot were playing,' Jean said. 'We'd have sorted you out, wouldn't we, girls.'

The women pumped their fists and cheered. 'Too true.' 'You bet.' 'No contest.'

'Dream on,' Duggan said. 'We'd have run rings round you lot. Still could.'

'Diamonds versus coal dust,' Spike said.

Some of the women cocked their thumbs at Brian's two friends. One of them asked the pair if they'd looked in the mirror lately.

'If you were playing in my front garden, love, I'd shut the curtains,' Duggan said, and he downed the last of his drink.

'You think you were good,' Jean said. 'That was then. We're good now.'

Duggan and Spike didn't respond. They were already on their way to Brodworth town centre for the afternoon session.

'Tossers,' Jean said, and her team cheered.

'They don't mean any harm,' Brian said. 'They're good lads really.'

'They don't mean any harm? Is that why you didn't defend us?'

Brian was in the dock, the whole team waiting for his reply. Why was he suddenly the villain?

'It's not aimed at you and your team. They've got a couldn't-care-less attitude about everybody and everything. And why not. Life can be cruel.'

'There are too many couldn't-care-lessers about,' Jean said, and she picked up her clipboard. 'I need to be off, girls. I'm covering the late afternoon shift. Well done. That was a good session.'

'I might see you later,' Brian said, stepping out of her way. 'I'm visiting my dad this aft.'

Brian sounded his horn and his brother Jeff came rushing out of the house without looking back. Jeff's wife, June, standing motionless and unsmiling at the window, watched every move her husband and her brother-in-law made. Jeff quickly put his seat belt on but Brian took his time, adjusting the rear view mirror, checking he was in neutral before gently selecting first gear. He wasn't going to rush just because June was staring coldly at both of them. Why should he let June dictate how he behaved? He wasn't as soft as Jeff.

'I take it you haven't told June what we're doing today.'

'No. Not yet. I will. She's getting a bit suspicious. I've got to be careful.'

'You need to get a grip, Jeff. How long are you going to let this go on?'

Their dad's house was a half hour drive away. They were ten minutes into the journey and they still hadn't spoken to each other. All this secrecy. Jeff more interested in himself than their dad. Brian sneaked a look at his brother's profile. He looked sad, hunched over, mouth turned down. Had he upset him? Had he been too blunt, telling him to get a grip? Did that make him a couldn't-care-lesser, no different to Duggan and Spike? Jean's words kept coming back to him, knocking him down.

'I bumped into Tommy Duggan and Spike earlier on,' Brian said.

'I'll bet that was painful.'

'They've not changed.'

'Somebody said they'd seen Duggan outside his house the other day arguing with himself.'

'We got talking about the old Acorn days.'

'Right.'

'I might try and organise a reunion.'

'Why not.'

'First and second teams.'

'When are you thinking of having it?'

'I don't know. When I get some spare time from all this stuff I'm doing for my dad.'

They didn't speak again until they were parked outside their dad's terraced house. The house was built of sandstone which had darkened over the years. The net curtains in the bay window and the upstairs windows had faded. There were sawn off stubs of iron bedded in lead in the low stone wall along the front of the terrace, remnants of the railings taken for the war effort. A red and white plastic For Sale sign had been screwed to the low grey wall. It was bright and optimistic and not straight. Neither brother was in a hurry to get out of the van.

'It feels weird sitting here seeing our old house up for sale,' Brian said.

'Do you remember when we used to play shots in on that little patch of grass under the front window?'

'My dad used to go off his head when he kept finding all those divots in his lawn. He thought it was the rabbits from the railway banking.'

Brian unlocked the front door and picked the junk mail off the floor. The leaflets were cold and damp, especially the glossy ones advertising pizzas and blinds, and he stuffed them into a black plastic bag at the bottom of the stairs.

'Let's start in the bedrooms. I left some cardboard boxes and plastic sacks up there the other day after I'd cleared out the wardrobe.'

Brian clicked the light switch for the upstairs landing and the downstairs hallway light came on.

'All the years I lived here and I still haven't worked out which switch is which.'

It was an opening for a witty response but Jeff stayed silent and followed Brian up the steep narrow stairs. Brian opened both bedroom doors to let some light into the tiny landing and then clicked the light off, a reflex action drilled into both of them by their mother to save the pennies. Jeff froze on the top step and stared at the ceiling. Brian tracked his gaze to the crimson lampshade with its matching tassels, the cracks in the plaster and the finger marks around the loft hatch.

'Are you alright, Jeff?'

'I'm not looking forward to this.'

'Me neither. It's no fun looking through all these cupboards and drawers. In and out of the rooms. Floorboards creaking. It's spooky.'

'I haven't told June my dad's gone into a home.'

'Bloody hell, Jeff. You'll have to tell her one day. I'm having to do everything.'

Brian opened the bedroom window and a current of fresh air cooled his face.

'It's a full time job trying to keep on top of all the stuff I get from the home and the local authority, the bank, the pension department. You wouldn't believe the number of forms I've had to fill in since my dad went in, and it's not done yet. The last one I did for the local authority took me four hours. I've been keeping a log of everything I've done over the last three months. Forms, phone calls, letters, face to face meetings. Everything. Do you know what the tally is? Go on, guess.'

Jeff shook his head.

'Three hundred and counting and God knows how many hours. It's a bureaucratic nightmare. How old folk cope on their own, I've no idea. Then the final insult is they want to take the old lad's house off him.'

'I know, Brian. I know. It's not fair. My dad's worked all his life, paid all his taxes, and then because he gets a brain disease he's left all on his own. If he had a different illness he'd be taken care of all the way through to the end. Cradle to grave.'

'It would be a great help if you could give me a hand with the house sale. That's all. I'd do everything else. Just help me sort out the estate agent, and the utilities, and the solicitor, and the post office. It's a nightmare.'

'I wish I could give you a hand, Brian. But if a letter came to our house with my dad's name on it, and June found it, she'd throw me onto the streets.'

The catch on the linen cupboard above the hot water cylinder wouldn't release, and Brian had to yank the door open.

'I feel guilty about that door. My mother asked me to fix it just before she went into hospital for the last time and I never did. It's only a two-minute job.' Brian pulled out a stack of folded blue bed sheets and handed them to his brother. 'Are these any good to you?'

'Not really.'

'I didn't think they would be. I'll take them to the charity shop.'

Together they went through the drawers and cupboards in the two bedrooms and put all the items fit for the charity shop into cardboard boxes, and all the items of no use to anybody into black plastic bags.

Brian had already emptied everything in the kitchen on his last visit, and now he led Jeff into the front room and they tackled the cupboards and shelves.

The drawers in the sideboard were full of utility bills and instructions on how to operate every gadget in the house; from the TV remote, to the telephone, to the room thermostat. Underneath the documents, Jeff found a bundle of old Christmas, birthday and anniversary cards filed in chronological order and tied together with pink yarn. He turned away, head down, and handed the pack over to his brother.

'Do you want these? They're all from you and Susan.'

Brian flipped through the cards. Not one from Jeff and June. What the hell had caused all this?

'No. Bin them. They don't mean anything to me.'

When the drawers and cupboards in the sideboard had been emptied, and all that remained was grey dust, fluff, white bug powder and the old yellow newspaper lining, Jeff noticed a photograph sticking out of the back of one of the drawers.

'Look at this. I've never seen this photo before.'

They both held onto a corner of the photograph, not wanting to be the first to let go, and smiled at the happy faces of their young mother and dad walking along the sea front hand in hand, Brian and Jeff skipping along by their side.

'I can only have been six or seven then,' Brian said. 'You would have been four or five.'

'I don't remember it. Where was it taken?'

'Skeggy I think. We went to Skegness every year for feast week when we were young.'

They went through the rest of the house, filling sacks and boxes and finally there was only the cubbyhole under the stairs to empty. The gas and electricity meters were housed there and there was always a smell of gas. It was a cramped, dark place. Brian once locked Jeff inside when they were playing hide and seek. His brother screamed so loud their mother came running in from the back garden

11

to see what had happened. She threatened to give Brian a cuff round the ear and then told Jeff to stop crying.

Jeff pulled out a pile of coats and at the back he found a pair of football boots. 'Now then, what have we got here?' He held the heavy brown leather boots by their long laces at arm's length and watched them turn slowly and settle. 'My granddad's old football boots. Why has my dad kept hold of these for all these years?'

Brian put his hand inside one of the hard boots.

'I wonder if that's why he's always talking about playing football with my granddad. He says it every time I visit him.'

Jeff tried to bend the leather sole, its six leather studs worn down to the nail heads, but it wouldn't flex.

'They must have meant something to him, because I remember he kept putting them back under the stairs whenever my mother threatened to throw them in the bin when she was tidying up.'

'I think my dad thinks you and me's still at school. The other day he said he was going to bring my granddad to watch us play football for the school team.'

Jeff stopped trying to bend the stiff sole.

'Did he actually say my name?'

'Clear as a bell.'

Jeff smiled for the first time that afternoon. Brian put the boots and the Skegness holiday snap in a carrier bag.

'These are going to the home with us.'

Woodland House car park was empty and Brian parked the van in his favourite space in front of the laundry room. He took his seat belt off. Jeff didn't.

'What's wrong?'

'I can't do it, Brian.'

'Oh for...Come on, Jeff. You've come this far.'

'I can't. I'm still not ready. Leave your keys. I'll wait for you in the van.'

Brian clenched his teeth and glared at his kid brother. It was like looking at himself. At school people used to get them mixed up, which came in handy whenever Brian was accused of doing something wrong. Even now, despite Jeff's full head of black hair and soft office fingers, and Brian's greying locks and calloused hands, people still mixed up their names. But the two of them were nothing like each other when it came to taking on responsibility. Totally different. Why couldn't Jeff share the load for once?

'All this way for nothing. Again. I'm disappointed in you, Jeff.'

'I'm disappointed in myself.'

Brian squirted sanitiser onto his hands, signed the visitor book, and took the little lift to the first floor. His dad and most of the other residents were asleep in the lounge. He put the Skegness holiday snap on the bedside table of his dad's room and came back into the lounge.

Gloria, one of the care workers was putting a clean pair of socks on the feet of Arthur, a resident, talking to him all the time, gently straightening his legs which were folded up tight against his chest. On her forearm Gloria had a tattoo of a motorbike being ridden by a figure in leathers, the blue and black ink sharp against the carer's pale skin. Arthur was moaning, eyes clamped shut, and the effort had pushed his black safety helmet off-centre.

Jean, the senior care worker came into the room with her head up, checking to see if everyone had finished their afternoon tea and biscuits, chatting briefly with those who were still awake. Brian took the football boots out of the carrier bag and held them in the air by their long laces.

'Have you seen these, Jean? They're my granddad's old football boots.'

Jean turned the boots over and tapped them together, stud to stud.

'They're in good condition.'

'I thought my dad might enjoy messing about with them. Something to keep his mind working.'

'That's a great idea.'

'And it might bring back some memories of his playing days as well as memories of my granddad. Would that be okay?'

'Absolutely.'

Brian took the boots back off Jean and carefully placed them side by side between his dad's feet.

'It looked like you'd had a good training session in the park when I saw you earlier on. I didn't know you were into football.'

Jean paused in the doorway and squirted sanitizer on her hands.

'We had a great session, didn't we Gloria,' she said, rubbing her hands dry.

'Yes. It was tough. Bloody hard. She's a slave driver.'

'Eight turned up,' Jean said. 'Six from here and one each from the other two care homes. That's not bad considering the shift patterns we work. We've got the makings of a good seven-a-side team.'

'You take your football seriously.'

'We do. When you work as hard as these girls work you have to play hard as well. Otherwise you'd go under. We were practising penalties and Gloria turned out to be our best penalty taker. She'll not admit it but it's true.'

Arthur gave a low cry when Gloria succeeded in straightening out his legs. Her freckled hands were as pale as Arthur's legs and when she looked up and thanked Jean for the compliment, her face was flushed.

'We're like a stable of thoroughbreds,' Jean said. 'Pent up and ready to go. We just need a good seven-a-side team to play against. We've played a few games in the park against friends and family but we'll never improve until we find some good opposition to play against. A team that'll test us.'

'I've been thinking about organising a reunion of my old football team, the Acorn. I haven't seen half of them in years.'

'Good for you.'

'If it comes off I could see if any of them fancy pulling their boots on again.'

'I'm liking the sound of this.'

'I could have a go at putting a seven-a-side team together. An over fifties team.' Brian laughed at his own suggestion. 'We could play your team of carers.'

'What a match: young versus old, women versus men, carers versus couldn't-care-lessers.'

Brian took a step back and tried to keep smiling. Jean's summary of him and his old teammates was less a straight jab to the eye, more a tweak of the nose.

'We're not all couldn't-care-lessers. There were some decent lads in that team. It would be a good match.'

'I'm already ahead of you. I can see it: A village affair. A Saturday afternoon spectacle in the park. A seven-a-side decider.'

'They'd take some persuading after all these years,' Brian said, and he patted his beer belly. 'We'd have to get fit first.'

'You can do it, Brian.'

A tall woman, in her mid-twenties with shoulder length fair hair came into the lounge spinning a yellow soft football on the tip of her long, slender index finger.

'Stand back,' Jean said. 'It's play time. You've not met our new activities coordinator and soon-to-be Carers United goalkeeper have you Brian. This is Kalina. She plays in goal for Masons FC seven-a-side women's football team on Sundays and she's going to play for us during the week.'

'Masons FC are from Sheffield,' Kalina said. 'We are a good pub side. I have heard all about your dad, Brian. Jean says he used to be a goalkeeper like me.'

'You wouldn't think so looking at him now but when he was playing he was fearless. He was known to his team mates and opponents as The Tiger.'

It could have been coincidence but at the mention of the word tiger Brian's dad opened his eyes and smiled.

Kalina bounced the football a few times and slowly all the residents woke up, smiled, and reached for the yellow ball.

'Right, Joe. Your turn first.'

Kalina tossed the soft ball to Brian's dad and asked him to catch it and throw it back. But the old man sank in his chair and began to cry. Brian rubbed his dad's arm.

'It's okay, Dad. It's only a bit of fun. It's just a game.'

The air in the room was hot and bending down to retrieve the ball had made Brian sweat. The temperature didn't appear to affect Kalina. She had that pale Polish complexion that doesn't tan easily, and there wasn't a hint of heat on her fair cheeks.

'Come on, Joe. Give me a big smile.'

Brian's dad let go of the arm rests when he saw Kalina spin the ball on her finger and he reached out to her. Brian clapped, partly in appreciation of Kalina's ball skills and partly at the joy of seeing the sparkle return to his dad's eyes.

'That's it, Dad. You show them how good you were.'

Kalina tucked her hair behind her ears and tried again. This time Brian's dad tracked the ball's flight and caught it on its way down. But instead of throwing it back, he kicked it into the air with such force his slipper flew off. There was only one ceiling light in the room and the ball found it.

Mary, sitting at the side of his dad screamed and cried as a hail of plastic fragments fell onto the carpet in front of her. Arthur drew his knees up to his chin again and closed his eyes.

Brian jumped off his stool, laughing, trying not to punch the air.

'Bloody hell, Dad. Go steady. Sorry Kalina.'

He recovered the slipper from behind the TV and gently eased it back onto his dad's foot. Jean asked Aisha, another care worker to help Kalina clean up. Aisha, in her early twenties and tiny at under five foot, was happiest keeping her head down vacuuming, whereas Kalina, towering over her colleague, took up every inch of her six foot frame.

When they had finished, Aisha turned the vacuum off and in the silence that followed, Mary reached out and stroked the young care worker's cheek.

'What beautiful black skin you have my dear.'

Aisha smiled and wiped away a tear from Mary's cheek.

'Thank you, Mary. You have beautiful skin too.'

Brian pulled his T-shirt away from his chest and blew a sharp blast of air into the gap making the cotton flutter.

'Do you mind if I open the window for a minute, Jean? I'm not used to all this activity.'

The leaves on the tree in the back garden of Woodland House were motionless in the afternoon heat. As Brian reached for the window handle a flock of starlings dropped out of the sky and disappeared into the tree's dense foliage. He gave them a few seconds to settle then slowly opened the window. The birds must have been watching and as the security chain reached its limit they flew out of the tree as one. When Brian turned back round all the residents were asleep again and Aisha had left the room.

'Aisha plays up front,' Jean said. 'I know she doesn't look big enough to be a striker but she's brilliant. When she plays well the whole team play well. She didn't think she was good enough to be in the team when she first started here, but she's soon settled in. I keep telling her not to put herself down. We don't do wallflowers here.'

'Aisha looks like a flower ready to bloom,' Kalina said.

'That's a good description.'

'Good luck getting the old Acorn team back together, Brian,' Jean said. 'That's your challenge for the week. We'll be ready for you. Now will you excuse us, I need to talk to Kalina and then I've some paperwork to catch up on.'

Brian smiled to himself in the lift on the way out. Jean's attitude bordered on over-confidence, but there was no swagger or cockiness in her opinions. He was still smiling to himself as he stepped into the car park. 'My challenge for the week is it?' he said out loud. It was the first time a woman had challenged him in five years. Maybe that was why he was still running his fingers through his hair when he got to his van.

As he was opening the van door a woman cried out for help from somewhere on the first floor of the care home. One of the bedroom windows was open a few inches to the limit of its chain but he couldn't see anyone. He slid

18

into the driver's seat and Jeff closed the newspaper he was reading and threw it onto the dashboard.

'Who the hell's making all that noise? They sound as though they're in pain.'

The woman's plea for help sounded more heart-breaking with each cry.

'I don't know. It happens. Somebody'll come and help her in a minute. They never leave anybody in distress.' Brian put his seat belt on and started the engine. 'Come on. Let's get you back home before June gets even more suspicious.'

'How was he?'

Brian turned the engine off and faced his brother.

'You really ought to have come in with me, Jeff. You'd have enjoyed it.'

Jeff stared out of the window, hands squeezed tight between his knees. The silent gaps between the woman's mournful cries lengthened and then the crying stopped all together. As if waiting its turn, a dog began to bark from somebody's yard at the back of the terraced houses behind the care home. Brian smiled to himself as he recalled the shattered ceiling light and the cheeky grin on his dad's face.

'He was even showing off his ball skills.'

'His ball skills.'

'He brought the roof down. It's frustrating. He was fast asleep when I visited last week – never opened his eyes. Then he was wide-awake the other day. I put that Matt Monroe tape on, the one my mother said they used to listen to when they were courting. Remember? My dad got up smooching with one of the care workers. You ought to have been there.'

'Smooching.'

19

'It was funny. We were all laughing our heads off. And then 'Softly As I Leave You' came on and I nearly cracked up. I had to get out of the room.'

They left the car park and waited in a queue of vehicles to join the busy high street. To merge with the speeding cars and lorries inches away from mothers and pushchairs. To avoid the pull up and drive off delivery vans parked on yellow lines, hazard lights flashing. To be reflected in the shop windows, passing through shoppers looking for a bargain or somebody to talk to.

'We're only two hundred yards from Woodland House and it's like entering another world,' Brian said. 'It's a time warp. I tell you what, Jeff. Better make the best of this world, as mad as it is, because there's a good chance it'll not be long before you and me are in that other world of catch-the-ball-and-throw-it-back.'

'If I go first, bring me a magic pill and a can of lager.'

'There's a resident in there. Arthur's his name. He can't be much older than you and me.'

'Jesus.'

'He has fits and he has to wear a safety helmet all day long. He's fast asleep most of the times I see him. Nobody visits him. No family. No friends. Nobody.'

'Poor bastard.'

'And one of the women, Mary, she used to be a headmistress. One minute she's crying and asking for her mother to come and take her home and the next minute she's back at school teaching a classroom full of kids.'

'I wonder what's going through my dad's head.'

'Who knows, Jeff. That's the problem.'

'I will try and visit him. I promise I will.'

'Time's ticking by.'

2

Brian scraped the razor down his cheeks and over his chin then swished the blade clean in the bowl in the kitchen sink. His skin, magnified by the little round mirror on the windowsill, looked smooth and shiny and made the bags under his eyes stand out. He swivelled the mirror, shutting his eyes for a second as the glass caught the flash of morning sun, and lifted up his fringe. He could place all four fingers sideways in the gap between his eyebrows and his hairline these days. Either his hand was getting smaller, or he was losing his hair faster than ever.

He made himself a cup of coffee and a slice of toast. The news item on the early morning TV had shifted from tensions in the Middle East, to a cat returning home after being thought lost for three years. He muted the sound and in the silence stared at the pine dresser in the alcove opposite the sink. The shelves were full of delicate cups and saucers, and there was a photograph of himself, hair thicker and darker, and his wife Susan on holiday in Spain. He wiped the thin layer of dust off the top edge of the silver frame with his finger.

'Well, Susan my love. You'll never get any older.'

He put the photograph back in its place on the dresser, and took the remains of his toast out to the bird table. A starling landed on the ridge of the greenhouse and looked straight at him. The greenhouse, bare apart from a few empty plant pots and canes rotted black at their base and tied together with faded twine, looked dreary against the

21

bird's sparkling iridescent plumage. Back in the kitchen he emptied his cup down the sink. Susan would have got onto him for leaving coffee stains around the plug hole, expecting her to scrub the stainless steel clean when she got back from work. They would have had a little argument about him taking her for granted. Then they would have kissed and gone their separate ways to earn another day's living. What he would give to have those silly little tiffs every morning again.

As he looked out of the kitchen window, the starling, in one direct move, left the greenhouse, landed on the bird table, grabbed the toast, and flew off again with the meal clamped in its beak.

'Right,' Brian said out loud. 'That's it. Come on. Do something.'

He picked up his mobile.

'Hey up Malc. Fancy a pint at the Station tonight after work? I reckon it's time we organised a reunion of the old Acorn side.'

Brian sat on a bar stool at the Station Inn with his pint half drunk, waiting for Malc to turn up, thinking about his footballing days and the friends he had made over the years playing for the Acorn. It seemed to be a never ending age of beer, sandwiches and bonding. Players had found good jobs during that period – electricians at the Electricity Board, gas fitters at the Gas Board, brickies on the building sites and fitters in the factories. They probably bought their first house while at the club. Perhaps started a family. Maybe two-timed their wives. And the football team had been the thread that bound it all together.

Brian was back in the Acorn, passing round the trophies, drinking and cheering with the lads and he didn't see Malc until he was almost standing over him.

'I could have just nicked your pint and picked your pocket at the same time.'

'Sorry, Malc. I was miles away. It was Saturday night. We'd just done the double.'

'How many have you had?'

Malc bought them both a pint and they found an empty table in a quiet corner, well away from the giant TV screen.

'What's brought this on then?' Malc said.

'I thought it was about time I got off my backside and did something with my life again.'

'Well, I'll drink to that,' Malc said, and he forced a reluctant Brian to raise his pint and chink glasses. 'It's good to see you getting out again old pal.'

Neither of them mentioned Susan. Malc was a good friend, too close to Brian to risk embarrassing or upsetting him. Brian appreciated his friend's empathy. But it was just another day where no one talked about Susan. It never seemed to be the right day or the right place.

'What do you think about having a football reunion?' Brain said.

'I think it's a great idea. We should have had one before now.'

'It must be twenty years since we packed in.'

'It was two thousand,' Malc said. 'I know because everywhere you went all you could hear was Robbie Williams blurting out 'Millennium' and everybody joining in the chorus.'

'I was thirty that year.'

23

'After we folded it wasn't two minutes before just about every other club in Brodworth folded. They've virtually all gone now.'

'There's nowhere to play anymore,' Brian said. 'The council's sold off all the playing fields. They're all posh houses and business units now.'

'There's maybe half a dozen clubs left. Aspinal Rec and Worsley Park are still going from the original lot.'

'It's crazy. Half a dozen teams in a town the size of Brodworth. No wonder there's trouble on the streets. We used to vent our aggression on the field. Now the young kids would sooner pick up a knife.'

'*You* used to vent your aggression on the field,' Malc said. 'I was an angel compared to you.'

'You had your moments. I remember you scything down that winger when we played the Soldiers Arms. They had to carry him off.'

'He deserved it. He was faster than a greyhound.'

Malc was shorter and stockier than Brian. He wasn't very fast over five yards and to compensate had mastered a fierce tackle. Brian and his team mates used to call him the gentleman because, thankfully, he never used the frightening tackle in training. The name stuck and even now, Malc was known as the gentleman electrician.

Brian and Malc took a drink of lager to show there was no malice in the ribbing, and they made sure they put their pints back down on the table at the same time.

'Play your hardest to win,' Brian said, 'and then shake hands with everybody after.'

'Even with those you hated.'

'Especially with those you hated. But we never hated anybody really. We all respected each other.'

'Anyway, where are you thinking of having the reunion?'

'I'd have gone for the Acorn, obviously, if they hadn't turned it into a rug warehouse.'

'We could still go there,' Malc said. 'I can just see us all sitting round in a big circle on little Persian carpets looking like a load of Aladdins.'

'All in flat caps instead of turbans.'

'What about having it here? We could use the function room. It's big enough.'

'Fine. The beer's okay.'

'Pie and peas?'

'Good idea. I'll try and get a good deal.'

'When are you thinking of having it?'

'I don't know. Next month sometime?'

'Why don't we make a list of everybody we can think of who had anything to do with the Acorn, split the names between us, ring them all up, see what response we get, and if it looks like a goer, fix a date?'

'That sounds like another one of your excellent plans,' Brian said, and he stood up. 'I'll see if they've got a pen and some paper behind the bar – we might as well start making a list now.'

'Hang on,' Malc said, and he leaned to his left, took a notebook out of his back pocket, and slapped it down on the table. Then he straightened his leg, took a pen out of his trouser pocket, and winked at Brian. 'Always be prepared. Anyway, while you're up, it's your turn.'

Brian smiled to himself as he ordered the drinks. Malc was a calming influence. Always in control, always making lists, always consulting his diary. He was the one who booked the holidays every year. A happy foursome; Brian and Susan, Malc and his wife, Pauline.

Malc loved organising the breaks. He never made a mistake in twenty years. Even when he ditched his paper diary a few years ago and switched to using his mobile phone to arrange his life, he still never made a mistake. Brian was happier with a pen and paper. He had no time for all that electronic wizardry and social media stuff. All that screen watching, photo taking, trend following, needing to be part of the crowd, craving the latest gossip and app. Some people lived inside their phones. It was one step from being a robot as far as he was concerned. Malc laughed at him and called him a Luddite. Maybe he was but he didn't care. He clung onto his old Nokia and to hell with anybody who tried to get him to upgrade to a smart phone or whatever they were called these days. Phones are for talking to people and booking jobs.

Over the next half hour they made a list of all the names of those connected with the first and second team at the Acorn, and in total came up with twenty one players, two managers, one bag man and two regular supporters.

Malc tapped a couple of names on the list with his pen.

'Do you think Duggan will come?'

'He might, if he's in the right mood.'

'What about Spike?'

'Depends what planet he's on that day.'

'I'll let you ring them.'

They crosschecked each other's phone contacts and split the task of contacting everyone and then feeling pleased with themselves, had another pint.

3

'Come on Helen. Don't let Gloria beat you. Get those arms pumping. One more shuttle. I know it's hurting. Come on, you can do it. Excellent. Well done team.'

Jean, standing in front of the children's play area in Woodland Park, blew her whistle and asked the seven young women to form a circle around her.

'Okay. Let's loosen off now. Relax your shoulders. Shake your arms. Shake your hands. Shake your legs. That's it. Good. Now gently roll your neck. That's it. Round and round. Good.'

A middle aged couple strolled into the park from the car park end and waved to Jean. A relative of theirs was a resident at Woodland House. As Jean waved back, a gang of young lads on bicycles appeared from behind the bandstand and the couple had to step off the gravel path onto the grass to get out of their way. The six cyclists circled the squad and whistled and made fun of the effort the women were putting in, and the serious way Jean was conducting the training session.

The lad leading the two-wheeled parade around the squad let go of his handlebars and took a photo of the group with his mobile.

'Look at the kit they've got on,' he said. 'I've chucked better jogging bottoms and trainers in the skip.'

A lad in the middle of the gang copied the lead rider and took a photograph of the squad with his own mobile.

'Which team are you lot then tonight? Oxfam United?'

The bikers laughed and the lad at the back rode to within a few feet of Aisha and reared up on his back wheel.

'Make sure you smile when it gets dark, love,' he said. 'Otherwise you'll get knocked down.'

Jean made straight for him. He dropped his front wheel and rode back to his mates, looking over his shoulder and laughing.

'One more word like that from you Ryan laddie and I'll fetch your mother and tell her to wash your mouth out.'

Ryan's mates laughed at him and he tried to act tough.

'She's not in. Anyway, tell her if you want. I'm not bothered.' His mates laughed even louder.

The women formed an advancing line behind Jean and slowly the lads rode away, laughing, glancing over their shoulders, and rearing up on their back wheels all the way out of the park.

'Right, girls,' Jean said. 'Tonight we're going to practise shooting.' She placed two cones a few metres apart in the middle of the park playing area. 'Kalina and Sylvia will play in goal and face alternate shots. Kalina. We operate a buddy system in the team. Does Masons FC use one?'

'No. I have not heard of this buddy system.'

'What it means is everybody is paired up with a team mate and they support each other during training or when we're playing a game or having a team talk. Or even when we're having a drink afterwards.'

Sheila, a carer from one of the sister homes, pointed at Anne, a cook from the same sister home.

'We definitely support each other. Especially when you're buddied up with somebody who likes to drink as much as she does.'

Anne threw one of her wrist bands at Sheila and it came back just as fast and accurate.

Jean was used to Anne and Sheila's larking around. Their antics brought vigour to the training sessions. Anne always turned up with a carrier bag full of chocolate bars for everybody. Her party piece was throwing the goodies into her team mates' training bag from ten yards away, eyes closed. She rarely missed. Sheila was not the best player in the squad but she was the most athletic. Every time she scored a goal, which wasn't that often, she performed an elegant backward somersault followed by a star jump. Anne once tried the manoeuvre and nearly knocked herself out. Although Jean had seen neither of them on duty at the their place of work, her fellow senior care worker at the sister home had assured her the two women were grafters and good fun to be around. Jean didn't need a report; she could tell they cared.

'We all support each other,' Jean said, 'but the buddy system is an extra layer.'

'I see. It is a way of getting close to someone and sharing thoughts and feelings.'

'I couldn't have put it better myself, Kalina.'

To begin with the shots were high and wide and only Helen and Aisha were on target. Tiny footed, seven stone Helen, could strike a ball so sweetly players turned their backs when she threatened to shoot, and whoever was in goal preferred to tip the ball over the bar rather than risk a sprained wrist trying to catch it. Everyone had great fun running after the ball, especially when it reached the kiddies play area and ricocheted off the slide and the roundabout and the swings like a giant pinball machine. Thankfully, no one, not even Helen, had a shot powerful enough to damage the distant bed of begonias or the bandstand.

For the next fifteen minutes, Jean coached the players on how to switch defence to attack and the evening ended with a competitive game of four-a-side, with Jean making up the numbers, and also refereeing. When she blew the final whistle, the players hugged each other, picked up their belongings, and set off along the gravel path towards the car park, reliving some missed shots and some great passes and goals. Jean stayed at the back, cones stacked inside one another under her arm, footballs in a net bag over her shoulder, talking to Kalina, Aisha and Sylvia, and Anne and Sheila from the sister home. Anne asked Aisha what job she did at Woodland House.

'I am a qualified care worker. I also have a responsibility for cleaning.'

Sheila said, 'You ought to be playing sweeper for us then if you're a cleaner.'

The two women laughed. Aisha smiled at first then looked down at the floor.

'I'm sorry Aisha,' Sheila said. 'It was just a joke.'

Aisha pulled the zip on her fleece tight up to her chin and Jean put her arm around her.

'Take no notice of these two. They have a different sense of humour to us at Woodland House.'

'We don't mean any harm, Aisha,' Anne said. 'You'll get used to us.'

'Well, Kalina,' Jean said. 'What do you think to Carers United?'

'You are very good. Very fit and fast. Especially Aisha.' Kalina looked down at Aisha and Aisha looked up at Kalina. 'You are a little rocket.'

'Yes she is,' Jean said. 'You're a natural, Aisha.'

'My grandfather used to play for the Nigeria national football team many years ago. He is my hero.'

'Wow,' Jean said. 'Did you hear that girls. We have international football blood in our ranks.'

Sheila and Anne put their thumbs up and Kalina placed her hand on Aisha's shoulder.

'It is a privilege to train with you.'

Aisha looked up at Kalina and they smiled at each other.

'And what do you think to our new goalkeeper, Aisha?' Jean said.

'She is like a gazelle. Very springy.'

'I'm glad my lad and his girlfriend told me about you, Kalina,' Jean said. 'How good you were with the kids at the play school. You were just the activities coordinator we were looking for at Woodland House.'

'Nathan is a very nice young man,' Kalina said. 'And Chloe and her little girl are very nice too.'

'Chloe seems pleasant enough and little Summer is lovely. But I'm not sure I'd describe my lad as nice. He's been in no end of bother with the police ever since he left school. He's nearly twenty and he causes me more trouble now than he ever did when he was growing up. But he seems to have settled down a bit since he met Chloe and little Summer. Well I'm hoping he has.'

Aisha said, 'A wild boy needs a wild girl to tame him.'

'Wise words, Aisha. Wise words. Anyway, Kalina. There is a place for you in our team if you want to join us. Sylvia is more than happy to play outfield.'

'I am,' Sylvia said. 'I'd prefer to play outfield than play in goal.'

'That is very good of you. I would enjoy playing here. The team is as good as Masons FC. I would like to play for both teams if that is possible.'

'Let me know who to contact and I'll try and arrange a friendly between us. You could play one game for us and one game for Masons FC.'

'Yes. Like I work two days for you at Woodland House and two days at the playschool?'

'That's right.'

'And three days with my brother at his Polish delicatessen.'

'Now I am impressed.'

Jean offered to walk with Aisha as far as the bus stop and wait with her until her bus arrived so she wouldn't be on her own. It would be getting dark soon, Jean said, and although the lads on the bikes they saw earlier on were only messing around, it was better to be safe than sorry.

'Would you like a lift home, Aisha?' Kalina said.

'No. It is okay. I will catch bus. It is no problem.'

'Where do you live?'

'My house is on Racecommon Road near the centre of the town.'

'Come on. I will give you a lift. I have just enough time before I go into work.'

'No. It is okay. I can catch the bus.'

'Okay. Good night everyone.'

Kalina drove out of the car park, and Jean and Aisha crossed the road and walked passed the shops towards the bus stop. There was no sign of the lads on their bikes. Jean looked at her watch.

'There's a bus into town in ten minutes.'

'Yes. I know it. Sometimes the driver talks to me.'

'Is somebody meeting you at the other end to walk you through the town centre up to Racecommon Road?'

'No. It is safe. I am not worried.'

'I'd be careful, if I was you. Especially at this time of night. Have you any relatives or friends who could meet you?'

'No. I am living on my own. I have a rented room. I know some of the other women living there. They are friendly, but I would not ask them to meet me. They do not like to mix outside with others.'

As they walked side by side along the high street Jean noticed their reflection in the shop windows. Jean was only five foot six tall, but she was an Amazon at the side of Aisha. The gentle care worker looked like a girl being taken to school by an adult. Jean tried to see the expression on Aisha's face but she kept turning her head away.

'That must be hard – living on your own.'

'I have no choice. It can be lonely but the other women in the house are there if I need them so it is okay.'

'Who do you rent the room from? Is it the council?'

Aisha stopped and looked down at the pavement. Jean put her arm around her.

'Are you okay, love? What's the matter?'

Aisha pulled a tissue out of her pocket and wiped her eyes.

'I miss my husband every day. He is not permitted to join me in the UK. I miss my mother and father every day as well. I am their only child. They are all back home in Nigeria. They cannot afford to visit me and I cannot afford to go back and see them. Not until I have earned enough money. But it will be a long time; my rent and my living costs take much of my money.'

So that was it. Jean had sensed there was something sad going on in Aisha's life. The way she hardly smiled. The serious, too serious, effort she put into her caring role at Woodland House. But the biggest clue was the way she suddenly appeared liberated and full of life whenever she played football. It was as though all her worries were stripped away as soon as she took off her little shoes and stepped into her football boots. And then when those little shoes went back on, the sadness returned.

'Come on. We'll miss the bus. Here's my mobile number. Ring me as soon as you get home. I mean it.'

'I promise I will. Thank you for caring, Jean.'

Up ahead, a man and a woman were waiting at the bus stop, the shattered remains of one side of the shelter strewn across the grass at their side. They said hello to Jean and nodded to Aisha but didn't smile at her. The woman asked Jean if Nathan was keeping out of trouble. Jean crossed her fingers.

'He was when I saw him this morning. Who knows what today will bring. This is Aisha. Aisha, this is Pat and Phil. We used to live next door to each other. Aisha works with me at Woodland House. And she plays football for us. She's our best striker.'

The couple smiled now and said hello and Pat leaned forward and asked Aisha to repeat her name.

'Aisha. That's a nice name. Where are you from, Aisha?'

'I have a rented house in Racecommon Road.'

Phil was about to laugh but he got a dig in the ribs from Pat. Jean told them Aisha was getting off at the bus station and would they keep an eye on her, because you never know who might be hanging around there.

'Of course we will, Jean. Aisha will be safe with us.'

Aisha got on the bus with the couple and they waved to Jean and she waved back.

4

Brian and Malc pinned the old photographs of the Acorn glory days around the walls in the function room at the Station Inn. It was Malc's idea to put them in a horizontal line six feet off the floor in chronological order. It was something he had seen on a visit to the art gallery in Leeds last year, he said. Brian raised his eyebrows.

'Is the Art Gallery a pub, then?'

'Don't you start.'

'I'm only kidding.'

Brian smiled. Malc wouldn't admit to visiting an art gallery to any of his other mates. They would repeat his words in disbelief, throw in a few expletives, and probably give him a floppy wrist.

'What did you go and see?'

'Some paintings by a bloke from Hebden Bridge. He was good. Me and Pauline went.'

They both turned away. Another dead end.

The photographs, most of them loaned for the evening by Col the Acorn's right back, looked as fresh as the day they were taken.

'I don't think I've got one photograph of my footballing days,' Brian said. 'I don't even know where my medals are.'

'Col's probably got them.'

'Where does he put them all? I thought he lived in a little terrace house.'

'They're in his garage with all his other footballing memorabilia. Hasn't he ever given you a grand tour? It's amazing. It's more homely than his house. He's lagged the tin roof and the walls. He's put plastic grass down on the concrete floor. Every wall's covered in photos. And he's put shelves up all the way round for all his trophies and medals. He's got hundreds. It looks amazing, especially when he turns the spot lights on.'

'What about damp? How does he keep everything from going mouldy?'

'He has a tiny electric heater on in winter, twenty four hours a day.'

'What's his missus say?'

'She doesn't mind. She's as keen as him.'

'Lucky man.'

Brian picked up the sheet of paper listing all those who said they were definitely coming to the reunion, together with those who said they would try their best but couldn't promise. Former miner Fred, the long serving magic sponge man, had already thanked Brian for inviting him, but said he wouldn't be able to get there because of his legs and he hoped they had a great time. Fred's voice had been shaky over the phone. The old stalwart would be eighty-plus now. The years really had flown by. Fred had a grip like a vice designed, the players suspected, to make them think twice about going down injured. Fred used to come into the changing room before the game to promote the 'meat draw'. No one knew where he got the raw meat from. Wrapped in plastic film on a white dinner plate, it looked like shovelled up road kill, and Fred would push the delicacy under each player's nose as they got changed for the game trying to entice them to enter the draw for the prize. It was probably one of the reasons Brian stopped eating meat. Apart from the occasional pork pie.

Brian checked his watch.

'It's knocking on, Malc. Where is everybody?'

Malc tapped the face on his big watch a couple of times and pressed the timepiece to his ear.

'It is Friday the eighteenth today, isn't it?'

Malc was kidding. He had never mixed up a date in all the years they had known each other. When they played for the Acorn, everybody used to poke fun at him whenever he took his diary out and made a note of an upcoming fixture or social event. But the ribbing never bothered him. All Malc did was wink at his tormentors and chuckle. Brian had a shorter fuse than Malc and the goading would have got to him. It always did, and he would have responded with a quick caustic reply and then regretted it.

They could smell the food before the waiters opened the doors, and brought in the two heavy trays of pies and the big stainless steel bucket of steaming mushy peas.

'It's to be hoped somebody does turn up,' Malc said. 'Otherwise you and me's going to have a beano with all this snap.'

Plenty did turn up, and by eight o'clock Brian and Malc had shaken hands, some warm and strong, others cold and weak, with seventeen former players and staff. Feeling happy with the turn out, they picked up a plate of pie and peas while there was still some left and split up to join in the laughter and reminiscing.

Some of the old gang hadn't seen each other for years. They scanned the room as they talked and laughed, checking who else was there, making eye contact across the floor and nodding. Occasionally they turned to a mate at their side, no doubt asking if that guy over there really was who they thought it was, or had he sent his dad in his place. Small groups formed and people chatted with those they felt most comfortable with. Malc told Brian he wanted to keep as far away from Duggan as possible, and he joined two lads standing in a quiet corner opposite the pie and peas table. Brian, feeling some responsibility for the event, decided to work his way around each group and find out how life was treating everyone. Steve, Alan and Ben opened up to let him join them.

'How's it going, Alan?' Brian said. 'Still keeping fit by the looks of it.'

Alan smiled a modest smile.

'Thanks, Brian. I keep getting out for a run.'

Steve cut in straightaway.

'It's because he's never done a hard day's work since he left school, that's why he still looks fit. Driving round delivering letters all day long.'

Alan continued to smile and he winked at Brian as if to say, here we go again. Alan was a calm, controlled footballer, always one step ahead of the man he was marking and he never broke into a sweat or needed to run more than ten yards to defend his area. Steve nicknamed him Dobbin the Gypsy Horse, because he played as though he was tethered to a post and only ventured as far as the invisible rope would allow.

Brian asked Ben how life was treating him. Ben was always a bit heavy as a player and now he looked three stone overweight. He ran his hand down his concave chest and out over his beer gut as though he was a proud mother-to-be.

'I'm full of goodness, Brian. It's the knees that's my problem. If I bend down to lay a row of bricks it takes me ten minutes to get back up again.'

Steve turned on Ben now.

'You've never bent down to lay a row of bricks in your life. I've seen you,' and he tapped the chair leg a few times with his foot. 'You've got a City and Guilds in toe end trowelling.'

'And how's Steve?' Brian said. 'Are you still living up Sheffield Road?'

'Not for long I'm not if they keep putting all these foreigners up there. They've taken over Racecommon Road. It'll be Sheffield Road next. It's amazing how quick they can find houses for all these migrants that's swarming all over this country. But try and find some houses for our lot and there's never any available. Funny that.'

'Now then, Steve. That's a bit racist.'

'It's not racist, Brian. It's true. You'll see one or two of them now and then, the women, in the back yards, nattering, looking over their shoulders in case they're missing something, all the time in the world. Then they disappear back inside when the big boss turns up in his black sunglasses and his big black BMW with its tinted windows. They're all criminals and spongers. I'd send the lot back.'

'There's plenty of criminals and spongers among 'our lot' as well,' Brian said. 'Especially the higher up you go. What about all them?'

'Send them back as well.'

Ben smiled at Brian.

'Don't get him going. He makes Enoch Powell look like Mother Teresa.'

Steve's face hardened and he wouldn't look at anybody.

'They should bring back Margaret Thatcher. She'd sort them out.'

'Mmm. Interesting,' Alan said, and he took a sip from his half pint glass. 'Wasn't it Margaret Thatcher who sold off all the council houses? Maybe that's why we have a housing shortage.'

Alan winked at Brian; not taking the mickey out of Steve, more like putting an arm around his shoulder to calm him down.

'It was one of the best things Maggie ever did,' Steve said. 'Selling off all the council houses. It made people go out and work for a living, and it got rid all those idle council workers sitting around in union meetings or having a day off because they'd got a little bit of a head cold. Now we've got all these foreigners coming over here and taking all our jobs.'

Brian shook his head. How had Steve's light hearted repeating of comedians' jokes all those years ago turned into a fear and hatred of people coming here from another country?

'You know I'm right,' Steve said. 'You've only got to look at the state of the town centre. It's full of druggies and layabouts. And none of them's from round here. They're all from Eastern Europe and Africa and Pakistan and God knows where. They don't mix in with the locals who've lived here all their lives. They all live in little communities. Everywhere's a no-go area. You need a passport to get into some of the streets they've taken over.'

'Talking of passports,' Ben said. 'Bad news about Benidorm. They've shut the Yorkshire Pudding bar. We'll have to find somewhere else for a pint now.'

'We'll find an English pub somewhere,' Steve said. 'I'm not drinking any of that Spanish crap and listening to all that foreign gobbledegook. I want to booze with people who speak the same language as me.'

Brian exchanged a few less controversial views with Alan and Ben about the shock of losing an old footballing

40

friend, who had died of a heart attack a few months ago, aged fifty five. This led on to keeping fit and the benefits of jogging (Alan) and drinking beer (Ben). Steve's angry face eventually softened, and he joined in the conversation again when they started talking about football and the good times at the Acorn. They were laughing and joking by the time Brian picked up another pork pie and moved to the next group where Phil, hands and mouth working together, was describing something to Col and Stuart.

'Glad you could make it, lads.'

Col licked his shiny spoon clean.

'It was the pie and peas that swung it.'

Brian hadn't seen his three old mates for years and they were grey and chubby. All three looked shorter. Stuart, who used to be over six foot when he played centre forward, had developed a slight stoop and now he was no taller than Col and Phil. Brian, conscious of his own bad posture, recited to himself the mantra his granddad, a sergeant in the army, used to drill into him; chin in, chest out, shoulders back.

Phil was waiting to continue his story.

'I was just telling Col and Stuart about that goal I scored against the Star Inn in nineteen ninety-six. Everybody said it was the best goal they'd ever seen at that ground. Do you remember it, Brian?'

Brian shook his head. Col and Stuart moved to one side and started up a separate conversation.

'I got the ball in the centre circle. It came to me at knee height and I took it down with the inside of my right foot like this and turned in one movement.' As he tried to demonstrate the elegant half-turn, he almost spilled his peas onto his jeans, the same brand and colour of jeans he used to wear in his twenties. 'I remember it as clear

41

as yesterday. I still don't know how I did it. Then I sent this beautiful pass with the outside of my right foot and the ball curled round their defence straight to Col's feet. Didn't it Col?'

Col didn't hear or maybe he chose not to hear and Phil kept on going for goal.

'I ran through the defence screaming for the ball and when Col crossed it, I volleyed it with my left foot like this, and it screamed into the back of the net. From leaving my foot to hitting the back of the net the ball never lifted more than six inches off the ground. I caught it that sweet I didn't even feel it and it never even spun. It was like a missile. Even their crowd applauded.'

A little shiver of delight rippled down Phil's shoulders. Maybe that was the only pleasure he got these days. He said he had also scored a great goal the season before and, smiling at the memory, said he would come to that in a minute. In the meantime, he wanted to tell Brian about his all-time favourite pass, and then he remembered a great header he'd once scored. He told Brian to remind him not to forget to tell him about that one. Brian listened to the monologue for a few more minutes and then, unable to find a gap, butted in and apologised for being rude and said he needed to have a quick word with his brother Jeff before he left.

The two lads Jeff was talking to looked familiar, even allowing for the passage of time. Were they former players? Supporters? Brian put his hand on Jeff's shoulder and told him he had just rescued him from death by a thousand goals. His brother was glad to have helped him out, even though he had no idea what Brian was talking about.

The two lads with Jeff were standing directly under the pub's bright fluorescent ceiling lights, and Brian saw something familiar in their eyes and in their smiles, but he still couldn't identify either of them. He screwed up his face.

'Don't tell me. It'll come to me.'

They made him suffer for a few seconds and eventually Jeff gave him a clue.

'You see how easily these superstars forget us, lads.'

Brian threw up his hands. Of course. The second team. Jeff was the goalkeeper for the second team.

'Bloody hell. It's Roger and Tim. Sorry lads. I should have known.'

'We know our place,' Tim said. 'Second team: second rate.'

Brian exaggerated how good the second team were, and how much the first team depended on them. Roger said nothing, Tim tried to smile, and Brian stopped rambling on.

Roger finished the second half of his pint in one go.

'The trouble with the way the Acorn was set up, with its first team and its second team, was that you lot thought all we wanted to do was play for the first team. We didn't. We were happy in the second team, weren't we?'

Jeff and Tim nodded. Roger's eyes were glassy and his voice was loud enough to be heard across the room. Duggan, standing next to Spike, was one of those in earshot, and he stared at Roger with that familiar dead smile that said he was beginning to get annoyed.

'In fact, we hated it when you took players from our team when you were short. We were trying to win our league. We couldn't care less what happened to you and your league.'

Tim leaned back out of Duggan's sightline.

'Keep it down, Roger. Let's not be upsetting anybody.'

'I don't care who I upset. I'm telling it like it is.'

Jeff said, 'It wasn't so much that we couldn't care less. I think it was more about keeping a happy team spirit together.'

'The trouble with most of you lot,' Roger said, sweeping his finger around the room, 'you thought you were better than you were. And you still do.'

Duggan, barrel chested and broad shouldered, hardly moved. But the warning signs were there: the red face, the looking away but seeing everything, the whisper to those standing next to him and the change in atmosphere those few words created.

When Roger and Tim went to the food table for a second helping of pie and peas, Brian tipped Jeff off about Duggan.

'I know,' Jeff said. 'I could sense it. Roger can get a bit bolshy when he's had a drink. I think him and Tim must have had a pint or two before coming here. But he doesn't mean half of what he says. When they come back I'll take them into the garden room round the back out of harm's way.'

'And I'll go and have a chat with Duggan. See if he's got any nice holidays planned.'

Before Brian could turn to go, Jeff held him by the arm. 'How's my dad?'

'He wasn't good yesterday. He was struggling with his breathing and they had to get the doctor out. Thankfully, the health centre's just around the corner from the home and the doctor came out straightaway. The doctors are great in that clinic. Jean can't praise them highly enough. My dad has to have an inhaler now. But he seemed alright when I left.'

Jeff was looking down at the floor and Brian wanted to tell him he really ought to visit soon, because you never know. But he had said it enough times, and it was now up to his brother. It was his choice. He was beginning not to care what Jeff did.

When Roger and Tim came back with their plates refilled, Jeff convinced them to join him outside for some fresh air while it was still light and Brian went over to talk to Duggan, Spike, and Duggan's unofficial chauffeur, Pete.

'Good do, Brian,' Pete said.

Spike laughed for some reason. 'It's a good night for dogs and kennels,' he said, and he grabbed Pete in a half nelson and only let go when his victim began to panic.

Spike had two personalities. It looked as though he had his weird head on tonight but it was difficult to be certain. It was impossible to work out which head was rising to the surface and which was sinking.

'What are you up to these days, Spike?'

Spike laughed to himself and then scowled just as quickly. Brian thought it best not to shake hands in case he got his fingers crushed.

'A bit of this. A bit of that. Nothing for you to worry about, my old cocker spaniel. My old sea dog. Still giving that red haired carer one? Hee ha. Never knock a carer; worth a fortune.'

'Fair enough, Spike. Whatever you say. How's it going with you, Tommy?'

Brian was greeted with a nothing-behind-the-eyes cold smile. Normal state. Duggan took a swig of his lager and wiped his top lip.

'Have a word with that mate of yours.'

'Who? Roger?'

'Tell him to shut it.'

'Tell him to stop wuffling,' Spike said. 'Wiffling and waffling.'

'He's just a bit loud. He doesn't mean any harm.'

When they were playing football for the Acorn there was always an uncomfortable atmosphere whenever Duggan came into the pub after the game. People drunk up and left. Others looked away and hoped he hadn't seen them. Those he caught out would smile and pretend it was good to see him, and chat and hope they could escape unharmed.

Brian couldn't work out why Duggan was so aggressive. It was a pity really, because he was the best goalkeeper in the league by a long way. He knew what he wanted from the players in front of him and, unless someone answered back, had the skill to get them to follow his instructions without upsetting them. He was totally committed to winning trophies and when he said someone wasn't good enough to be in the team, the coach would drop the player the next game. He also had a good sense of humour as long as he wasn't the one being laughed at. After he broke his back in training and ended up in a wheelchair, later on crutches, and now occasionally with a walking stick, he became even more aggressive and more isolated. Maybe the sudden loss of his dominant role as goalkeeper made him feel vulnerable. When the Acorn finally packed in you hardly ever saw him out.

'He was never any good,' Duggan said. 'He couldn't tackle. He couldn't head a ball. He couldn't shoot. That's why he never got in the first team. He played like a tart.'

Pete, who never played football and never missed a match, agreed.

'All the second team played like tarts.'

Pete would say anything to keep on the right side of Duggan, even when it was the opposite of what he believed. When the Acorn team was first set up, Duggan persuaded him to be the club secretary and a member of the committee and he made the most of Pete's easy going nature.

It was hard work talking to Duggan and hard work trying to ignore Spike's crazy interjections. When Pete took his car keys out and said it was time they were going, Brian went over to Malc and tapped him on the shoulder.

'Have you got a minute, Malc?'

'Sure.'

'Tell me if this is a silly idea. Do you think there'd be any interest in getting a team back together?'

'From the old Acorn?'

'Yeah.'

'I'm not sure about that. Have you seen the state of some of this lot? They've all on to play dead never mind play football. We've all put a bit of weight on.'

'I've already been challenged to a game.'

'Who's challenged you?'

'Jean, the senior carer at my dad's home.'

'Sorry Brian. I forgot to ask you. How is your dad?'

'He's fine, thanks. The old boy's being well looked after. He was a bit confused the other day when I visited him and I don't think he recognised me. The doctor told me dementia can be like that. One day they seem fine, the next day they seem to have slipped and then they come back again. He said it's like going up to a garden gate. The person stops and turns back, stops and turns back, and it can go on like that for a long time, and then one day they go through the gate and that's it, they're gone.'

'It must be tough.'

'It brings it home to you. It's made me realise you have to make the most of your loved ones while they're still with you. Anyway, as I was saying, Jean's put together a women's seven-a-side football team and they're looking for a good team to play against.'

'A women's football team!'

'I know. That's what I thought at first. But they're dead keen and by all accounts they're pretty good.'

'You'd never sell that to this lot. Have you been out with them on a Saturday night? It's like going on a pub crawl with Fatty Smith.'

'I know. Can you imagine what Steve would say to the idea. And Duggan and Spike.'

'Still, it might be worth a try,' Malc said, and he took the register of attendees out of his pocket and studied the names on the list again. 'The question is, are there seven players on this list fit enough and willing enough to pull on a pair of football boots again after all these years and play a team of women?'

'We can but ask.'

When it got to half past nine and the room was still full of people drinking and talking in little groups, Brian banged the back of a soup spoon on the pie and peas table, hard enough to create a little crater in the white table cloth. Malc shouted for order, and slowly everyone in the room stopped talking and turned to face them.

'Good evening everybody and thanks for coming. We weren't sure if anybody would turn up but it's been a good turnout for our first reunion.'

Malc said, 'We're thinking of making it a regular thing. Maybe twice a year. Before we all forget who we are and that we once played for the Acorn, the best side in Brodworth.'

Various comments were shouted out. A few were positive: 'What a good idea.' 'Let's make it four times a year.' 'Well done to you both.' But mostly they were mickey-taking: 'Mine's a pint.' 'Don't be so morbid.' 'Speak for yourself.' 'We're not pissing our pants yet.'

Brian gave a nervous laugh and said, 'There is another thing, lads, and no swearing. How do you feel about getting back together as a team? A new Acorn.'

There was laughter and then the room went quiet. People looked at each other and shook their heads. Even Steve was dumbstruck. Brian scanned the suspicious faces. Nobody looked familiar anymore; the greying hair, the beer bellies, the jowls and the shrunken statures. He was talking to strangers and the plan to form a team again and play a team of women didn't seem such a bright idea after all.

Roger, probably emboldened by another two pints and the absence of Duggan and Spike, was the first to shout out.

'Too old. Too late. Past it.'

Brian didn't want an argument to kick off, especially not on the first reunion, and he jumped in before anybody could respond to Roger's provocation.

'Somebody's already challenged us to a game.'

The old competitive spirit stirred and the silence changed to a low murmuring. Col asked Brian who had challenged them. Was it one of our old rivals? Alan said he would bet anything it was the Longbow Arms. Stuart agreed and said they always thought they were better than the Acorn.

'No. It's none of them. Don't laugh. It's a team of women.'

They did laugh. It broke the tension. Now everyone had a view:

'Are they young and fit looking?'

'Not too fit, I hope. My reputation could be at stake.'

'How can you tackle a chuffing bird? Stuff it – yes; tackle it – no chance.'

'If they're any good they'll not be women.'

'Look well if they're as good as the Lionesses.'

'Lionesses! You're kidding. Have you seen them play? I could walk straight into that England team today. Even with my dodgy knees.'

On it went. It was what he expected and it was disappointing. Malc felt the same. They waited for the jokes and the loud comments to subside and, when only a sceptical mutter came from the floor, Brian had another go.

'I can see nobody's rushing to put their name forward. We thought as much. But give it some thought. If nothing else it'll be a good reason to get fit again. Like we used to be when we were young and virile.'

'As Brian says, give it some thought. We'll ring round everybody over the next few days and take a view on whether it's got any legs.'

Steve shouted, 'If these women you're on about have got a decent pair of legs, you can put my name down now.'

The mood lightened, little groups formed and quiet conversations resumed, quiet enough for Brian and Malc to get a sense of how the suggestion had gone down.

Malc put his hand on Brian's shoulder and said, 'Make a sentence out of these four words: balloon, a, like, lead.'

5

Brian and Jeff drove into the care home car park and got out of the van together. All morning on the way to picking Jeff up, Brian couldn't get Jean's words out of his mind. Today he was determined to be a carer not a couldn't-care-lesser.

'How are you feeling, Jeff?'

'I'm okay.'

'You'll love it. Jean reckons my dad will be up dancing and singing.'

'Good.'

'They're a duo from Lost Harmonies. It's a charity dedicated to therapeutic music sessions for dementia sufferers. Jean said my dad loved it the last time they came to the home. I was working that day but I'm not going to miss it this time.'

Jeff was listening and at the same time scanning the upstairs windows. The woman they heard crying the last time they were there must have been on his mind. Brian opened the back doors of the van.

'Give us a hand with these scaffolding planks. I got them from the building site where I'm working. They were in the skip.'

'I believe you.'

'They're for Harry. That's him over there in the overalls with one of the residents.'

It was always a disappointment, the exterior of Woodland House. It wouldn't take much to put Jeff off.

51

The modern red brick walls and brown UPVC gave the front an austere look even in the morning sunshine. No projections or exposed lintels or contrasting sills to break up the façade. Cheap and functional. The hard working care home manager, a hero on low pay, had done her best to make the entrance welcoming. But the two plastic troughs and six plant pots she had placed on either side of the porch couldn't disguise the bareness of the outside of Woodland House.

Brian and Jeff carried the scaffolding planks over to Harry, the care home's volunteer handyman, who was showing a resident how to deadhead the plants in the troughs and plant pots.

'Morning, Harry,' Brian said. 'Are these any good to you? A gift to the home.'

'They certainly are. They'll come in very handy for the vegetable garden.'

'You're doing a grand job with the flowers.'

'Thank you. We'll soon have you pruning the bushes like a professional, won't we, Ronnie.'

Ronnie, who lived on the ground floor, took his broad brimmed straw hat off.

'Bush. Prune. Yes.'

Harry took the secateurs off Ronnie and told him to put his hat back on or else he would get sunburn.

'You love working in the garden, don't you, Ronnie.' Harry turned to Brian and Jeff. 'All the residents enjoy being in the garden. They look around and seem to go to another place.'

'My dad's the same. He loves it.'

'There's something true in that Andrew Marvell poem about gardens. A green thought in a green shade.'

Brian pulled open the entrance door and happy singing spilled out on to the car park.

'Here we go,' Brian said, and he nudged Jeff. 'We're all going on a... summer holiday. No more working for a... week or two.' His brother smiled but the warmth didn't reach his eyes.

'Come on then, Jeff. I'll sign you in.'

They had only got as far as the toilet round the corner from reception when an ashen faced Jeff stopped dead.

'Just give me a minute, Brian. I feel a bit uncle Dick. You go in.'

Brian stopped himself. Don't say anything. Be a carer today.

He walked on tiptoes and put his head around the door of the lounge. He stayed there half hidden, watching his dad and the other residents sing and dance with freedom and energy, wheelchairs no handicap, to the Cliff Richard song. The guitarist, a tall bearded young man with long ginger hair tied in a ponytail, and the singer, a woman about the same age, with thick brown curly hair wearing a necklace made of colourful beads were swaying to the beat of the song, encouraging everyone to join in. There was something magical in the air. The room had been transformed. Now the window was big and bright. The square of grey sky had turned blue. The rose buds on the curtains were in full bloom. The TV had shrunk. His dad's grey polo shirt dazzled. Even Arthur's black crash helmet had a jaunty, jazz look to it. Colour and light had entered the room. You wouldn't have known the residents were suffering from dementia. They were simply old and happy.

The headline of the Lost Harmonies brochure taped to the door at Brian's side read: 'When words fail, music speaks'.

He watched the whole performance from the doorway and only missed the minute it took to confirm Jeff had gone back to the van. When the session came to an end and the duo were packing up ready to go, Brian shook their hands and told them their music was better than any medicine. They thanked him in return and said it worked both ways.

The singer pushed her hand through her curly hair and straightened her colourful beads.

'As Mahatma Gandhi once famously said, the best way to find yourself is to lose yourself in the service of others.'

The duo waved goodbye and a few minutes later Arthur, Mary and most of the other residents were asleep. The few visiting relatives moved quietly into the dining room for tea and biscuits. Brian said he would join them in a minute and he sat down next to his dad and held his hand.

'Did you enjoy that, Dad?'

'It was okay.'

'They got you all going. You were singing along like there was no tomorrow.'

'Were we?'

His dad's eyelids began to close slowly and his eyes rolled upwards; then he opened them again and looked around the room as though he had never been there before.

'Shall I go and get you my granddad's old football boots from your room, Dad?'

His dad smiled and his eyes closed again. Brian fetched the boots, and the photo of the family holidaying in Skegness. He sat down and waited for his dad's heavy eyes to open again.

'Here you are, Dad. I brought these in the other day. Do you remember? They're my granddad's old football boots.'

His dad had a smile that said he didn't understand what was being said, but he was content. Maybe it was the medication. Or maybe it was a glimpse of his dad's old philosophical self, surfacing now and then from somewhere deep inside. Brian picked up the photograph and spoke softly in case his dad had fallen into a deeper sleep.

'Do you remember where this was taken, Dad?'

His dad's eyes half opened and he smiled that smile again.

'It was in Skegness. We were on holiday. That's you. That's my mother. That's me. And that's our Jeff.'

'Jeff.'

'Yes. Our Jeff, when we were kids.'

His dad's head began to fall forward and Brian gently lifted the football boots off his lap and took them and the photograph back to the bedroom.

As he was locking the door Jean came out of the lift with a grey box file in one hand, red ring binder in the other.

'Keeping an eye on things, Jean?'

'Somebody has to. Everybody else is having a great time singing and dancing.'

'That duo were brilliant. My dad loved it. Everybody loved it. It's amazing what a bit of music can do.'

'We've had musicians from Lost Harmonies a few times over the last few years and they've all been first class. We've had a violinist, a folk singer, a cellist, a flautist; that's a flute player in case you were wondering.'

'Cheeky. I know it's a flute player.'

'We contribute but it hardly covers their costs. They're worth every penny.'

'When everybody's singing and dancing it feels more like a club than a care home. It's not as intimidating a place as it first seems. I could give my time gladly if I could play an instrument. But I don't think they'd appreciate my comb buzzing and spoon tapping.'

'There is a limit.'

'Big night tomorrow. Me and Malc's set up a meeting with the old Acorn lads to see if we can put a side together.'

'Fantastic. Good luck with it. We're playing the pub side from Sheffield, the one Kalina plays for, next Tuesday night. The Masons Arms. I checked them out on their website. They're a seven-a-side team like us and they're good.'

'Are you playing them here in the park or in Sheffield?'

'In the park. Half past six kick-off. If it goes well, we might organise a rematch at their ground.'

'Excellent.'

'We don't have any goal posts or nets so they're bringing their own. It should be a cracking game. They sound as keen as us.'

'Half past six next Tuesday. I'll see if I can finish work early again. I might pop down and see how you get on.'

6

When Brian called to pick Jeff up on the way to the Station Inn, he didn't sound his horn and wait for his brother to come running out of the house, June standing at the window missing nothing. This time he parked out of sight and walked in full sunshine up to their front door. Having seen his brother sick with fear, unable to visit their dad to watch the Lost Harmonies live music, it was time to face his sister-in-law. It had to be done.

Neither Brian nor Susan, when she was alive, had spoken to June in years. He wasn't sure what had caused the rift. Some argument between June and their dad, that's all he knew. Jeff wouldn't talk about it. Jeff and June had stopped visiting his dad over thirty years ago, which was bad enough, but now with his dad living with dementia in a care home, the situation was beginning to drive Brian and his brother apart.

When June opened the door, she was smiling as though expecting a friendly neighbour or a parcel delivery. But the years of suspicion and animosity between the two of them quickly drained the warmth out of her face. She shouted Jeff's name. Her voice was flat. She glared at Brian, it can only have been for a second, but it was long enough to frighten him. She turned away and he was left standing with one foot on the doorstep, mouth open.

The polished wooden floor in the hallway sparkled and there was a welcome mat with an image of the sun above a field of daisies. There were no stray fibres from the mat and no sign of fluff or dust anywhere. Susan would have been envious.

Brian heard cushioned footsteps padding down the stairs.

'Hey up, Brian.' Jeff looked over his shoulder then straight past his brother to the road beyond the front lawn. 'Why didn't you sound your horn? I was ready.'

'I wanted to have a word with you and June before we got off.'

'What about?' Jeff glanced over his shoulder again and lowered his voice. 'Not my dad, is it? Is he alright?'

'He's fine. No. It's about me, but I suppose it's about my dad, as well. I think it's time I said sorry to June. It's gone on for far too long.'

Jeff took his jacket off the coat stand in the hall. 'I'm off, love. I'll be about an hour.' There was no reply and he stepped outside and closed the front door. 'Not yet, Brian. She's not ready.'

During the three mile detour to pick Malc up, Brian and Jeff talked about the weather and not much else. Malc was waiting for them and Jeff shuffled across to the middle seat.

'How's your dad, Brian?'

'He's doing alright. They look after him at Woodland House. The care workers are brilliant. I came across Aisha the other day. She's from Nigeria. She was sitting with my dad in a quiet corner next to the lift. He must have been panicking about something and she was consoling him, holding his hand, telling him everything was okay. She was great. The thing that got me, she didn't even know I was there. There were no other visitors around. It wasn't being done for show. It was genuine care.'

'I can see it affected you, mate.'

Brian took a deep breath.

'It did, Malc. When you have to put one of your family into a home, it's all guilt and doubts.'

Jeff sat back in his seat, out of the way of the flow of words between his brother and Malc, looking straight ahead, pretending to watch the traffic.

'I'd be the same if my mother or dad had to go into a home,' Malc said.

'You wonder whether you care enough. Could you have done more to keep them at home.'

'Brian. You couldn't care more. You're always talking about your dad. It was the same when Susan passed away. You've got to get on with your own life. You've got to keep on going, keep on working.'

'I feel I've let him down just when he needed me most. I want to try and repay him for all the sacrifices he made bringing me and our Jeff up, and for all the care he gave my mother over the years when she was ill.'

The van went round a sharp bend and Jeff held onto the dashboard.

It was only half past six and they had the pick of the tables at the Station Inn. Brian chose the one furthest from the big TV screen and Jeff bought the drinks.

'So, who's supposed to be coming tonight?' Brian said.

Malc took the list of those who said they were interested in getting back together as a team, out of his pocket and pressed it flat on the table between them. There was a red line through most of the names.

'Out of all those who came to the reunion only six have shown an interest. Your Jeff. Steve, believe it or not. Phil. Alan, as you'd expect. Stuart. And Col.'

'Six. Not many but better than expected.'

'Thank the Lord Spike's not put his name down.'

'If we could get one or two more we could pull together a seven-a-side team plus a couple of reserves. Seven-a-side's popular in the Sheffield area.'

'I could make one if we were really desperate.'

'Your knee's knackered.'

'I know.'

'Forget it, Malc. It's not worth the risk. I remember the agony you went through when you tore that cruciate ligament, and then all those months you spent hoping to get back playing again.'

'What about you?'

'My hamstrings will probably ping when I start running, but if I go steady and build up, I should be alright. But I was thinking it might be better if I did the coaching rather than playing. Unless you fancy it.'

Malc blew air out of his cheeks and shook his head.

'It's not my thing. Nobody would listen to me. They'd just take the piss. Can't we manage without a coach? We just need a captain on the field. We're all grown men now.'

The pub door opened and Steve and Alan came in. Jeff nudged Malc.

'Hey up. Here's half the back four.'

Steve accused Alan of lagging behind, and ordered him to get the drinks in for once, that's if he could find a few shillings in his purse without disturbing the moths. Alan smiled and winked and did as he was told.

'I'm glad you decided to give it a go, Steve,' Brian said. 'We didn't think you'd be interested.'

'Somebody's got to look after the old lad. He doesn't get out much. I'm thinking of registering as a child minder.'

Alan came back from the bar and put Steve's pint and his own half pint down.

'What's he been saying? Don't believe a word he says.'

'I was just saying I've got to get you back to the nursing home before it gets dark otherwise they'll be sending for the ambulance.'

Alan did his wink-smile and Steve did his usual good-natured laugh at his own failure to get a verbal response.

Alan asked if anybody else was coming. Malc turned the list round and pointed to the other four names. Steve tapped Col's name.

'I knew Col would put his name down. He's played for every team in Brodworth. He'll not want to miss out on playing in an over-fifties side. He's got more medals on his mantelpiece than Ryan Giggs.'

The pub door opened again and Col walked in with Phil. They got a drink and sat down at the next table. Phil read through the names of those they were expecting; Col took a photocopied photograph out of his jacket pocket.

'Anybody remember what year this was taken?'

Brian recognised himself as the long haired captain of the team with the trophy at his feet, Malc picked out his young, fit, long haired self on the back row, and Jeff picked out a surprisingly slim Duggan, the first team goalkeeper. They identified most of the players, but had no idea what competition the side had won or what year it was taken. Alan had a guess at the year.

'Nineteen...ninety...seven?'

'Correct,' Col said. 'We'd just won the Sunday League division one championship for the third year running. We beat Rowdon United three nil. Phil scored two and Brian scored a late goal with his head from a cross on the right.'

Brian said, 'Did I?'

A group of lads came into the pub arguing and laughing; the noise level rising. The door opened again, Stuart came in, bought a pint and sat down at Phil and Col's table. Despite the slight stoop he had developed over the years, Stuart still had the kind of shape and good looks designed to make a football shirt and shorts look tailor made. Back in their playing days, while everyone pulling on the Acorn team kit looked thin or heavy or short or gangly, Stuart would trot out onto the field looking like a model for a sports magazine.

'That's everybody, I think,' Brian said. 'Thanks for coming.'

Steve lifted a beer mat off the table like a trap door and looked underneath.

'Haven't you laid on any pie and peas for us? Alan's not eaten all day.'

'You'll have to make do with pickled eggs,' Malc said.

'Right chaps. The plan is to get back into playing again, get everybody fit and then maybe join an over-fifties seven-a-side league. There's one or two around – mainly pub teams.'

Col slipped the photocopy back inside his jacket pocket and rubbed his hands.

'Will we be joining a league with cup competitions and knock-outs?'

'Haven't you got enough medals, Col?'

'You can never have enough medals, Steve. A shiny silver over-fifties medal would sit nicely on the shelves in my trophy room.'

'We'll have to see. Malc's looking into it. The first thing is to organise a training session somewhere and see if the old magic's still there.'

Jeff asked who was going to be the coach. Before Brian could answer, the pub door opened. Col looked up.

'Speak of the devil.'

Malc folded up the list, muttered 'shit' and took a slow drink of beer.

Duggan, Pete and Spike got their drinks and sat down at the next table. Duggan was smiling at the floor, making no eye contact with anyone.

'We'd heard you were meeting here.'

'It's no secret, Tommy. Me and Malc are trying to get a team together.'

'That's right. We told everybody at the reunion what we were planning but I think you'd already left.'

'Absent birds eat little fish. Big fish have eagle eyes, don't they Pete,' Spike said, and he tried to pull Pete's earlobe off.

'I believe you,' Duggan said. 'How many have you got?'

Malc pointed to the six volunteer players around the two tables.

'This is it.'

'I can play, if necessary,' Brian said. 'We'd have a pretty decent seven-a-side team.'

'You should have told me from the word go. I could have got another six, couldn't I, Pete.'

'You could, Tommy; at least another six.'

Brian felt the mood shifting from good-humoured to watch what you were saying. How did Duggan do it? If you looked purely at his words there wouldn't be a problem. It wasn't what he said but the way he said it, daring you to have a different point of view.

Steve got up to get Alan the drink he owed him and Jeff did the same for Stuart. Buying your round suddenly became an urgent and important duty.

Alan said, 'We were just talking about having a training session. Let's see if anybody survives that trauma first before we go any further.'

Duggan said nothing until Steve and Jeff returned from the bar.

'Where are you going to train?'

'We haven't found anywhere yet,' Brian said. 'Malc's looking into booking a sports centre or something similar for an hour. It shouldn't cost us too much.'

Why did Brian always sound on the defensive whenever Duggan asked him a question? He should have shrugged his shoulders and kept his mouth shut, see what Duggan had up his sleeve.

'Leave that to me,' Duggan said. 'I've got my feelers out. I've got a good contact at Aspinal Rec.'

'Aspinal Rec?' Jeff said. 'They've got a great set up.'

'It'll be better than any fancy sports centre. And it'll cost us nothing.'

'A free for all,' Spike said, and he tried to squeeze Pete's leg. 'Keep hold of the pennies, Pete. Pennies make copper. Copper makes compounds. Compounds make interest.'

'Get off my leg, Spike. You don't know your own strength, man.'

Duggan ignored Spike's friendly attack on Pete and folded his arms.

'As I said, leave it to me.'

There were a few nods and a few quiet sips of beer. Duggan was the centre of attention and he was enjoying it.

Brian said, 'Like we mentioned at the reunion, if we do manage to get a team together, and if we do fancy playing a friendly against somebody to see if we've still got it, then we've already been challenged to a game. It's a seven-a-side women's team from my dad's care home in Clayton.'

Duggan's laugh was so exaggerated he nearly blew the froth off his pint.

'A seven-a-side women's football team!'

Spike opened his mouth wide and gave a silent scream.

'Don't hurt the little carers,' he said. 'Especially the dark ones. White man has to earn a crust.'

'By all accounts they've got a good squad,' Brian said. 'I'm going to watch them next week. They're playing a seven-a-side women's pub team from Sheffield. Masons FC. They're supposed to be a top side.'

Duggan wiped the tears running down his cheeks and shook his head.

'What a laugh. Two women's teams. I can't believe it.'

'A cake stand of girlie tarts and a little lodge of secret hand shakers,' Spike said. 'The game's gone bazookers, boys. Count me out.'

Alan spoke as though he hadn't heard Duggan or Spike's comments.

'What day next week, Brian? I might join you. You never know, we might get a surprise.'

7

Brian played for the Acorn against Aspinal Rec a few times when the two clubs were in the same league. At that time Aspinal Rec's ground was no better than most other grounds in Brodworth. There was a cold red bricked communal shower block with tepid water if you were lucky, windows with tin sheets nailed over the openings, a pitch marked out by volunteers or the council, broken glass and dog shit lurking in the grass. Aspinal Rec was lucky. It was one of the few teams to survive the gradual disappearance of local clubs at the end of the nineties and they had prospered and grown over the years.

Now, as Brian walked with the rest of the new Acorn squad along the tarmac path from the car park towards the club house, he saw a transformed ground. There were floodlights around the perimeter of the pitch and a covered stand with Blacks Builders, the club sponsor's name, painted in white on the corrugated roof. There was even a dugout to protect the coach and staff from over-excited supporters. The blades of the greenest of green grass looked identical, and the white lines marking out the pitch were as precise as those on a draughtsman's drawing.

'Bloody hell,' Brian said as he stepped on to the artificial turf. 'If only they'd had this pitch when we were playing I might never have hung up my boots.'

'Not bad is it,' Pete said. 'Tommy's come up trumps again.'

Duggan ignored the praise. The man couldn't take positive feedback; too hard for any of that nonsense.

'And that over there is the training ground,' Duggan said, pointing to an area about a quarter of the size of the football pitch with a ten foot high green wire mesh fence around it and scaled down floodlights. 'That's ours every Wednesday night and I've got the key to the gate.'

The players' footsteps made no sound on the soft, cushioned artificial turf. Alan bent down and ran his fingers through the synthetic grass.

'This takes me back to my days as a professional. We played on some superb pitches.'

Col slung his kit bag over his shoulder. It was the biggest and heaviest bag of them all.

'Yes, but how many medals have you got, Alan?'

Alan just smiled and winked at Col. Nothing got to him, on or off the pitch. You had to admire the man's calmness.

Steve asked Duggan where the changing rooms were.

'Use those benches at the top end of the training ground. They'll do.'

'Let's hope it doesn't rain.'

Duggan turned on Steve.

'Hey. Don't complain. This is the bees' knees.'

'I'm not complaining. I'm just saying I hope it doesn't rain. Alan's just had his hair permed.'

There were enough benches for everyone to claim a stretch of territory and the squad began to strip off and put on their training gear. Brian sat next to Stuart and watched him light a cigarette, place it on the edge of the bench and pull his kit out of his Asda plastic shopping bag. His black shorts and white T-shirt were scrunched up in a ball, and he had a black lace in one trainer and a brown lace in the other. And yet, when he was dressed, sitting there, leaning forward with smoke drifting up from the cigarette held loosely between his fingers, staring into space, waiting for everyone else to get changed, Stuart looked as cool as the rugged cowboy on the classic advert for Marlboro cigarettes.

Col had given himself plenty of room on either side of his bench for his clothes and all his training gear and he unzipped his big kit bag and laid everything out in a neat line. Steve nodded to Brian and one by one, unknown to Col, everyone watched him step out of his underpants and pull on his old jock strap, the same one he used to wear when they played for the old Acorn by the colour of it. Col began his preparations by wrapping a good yard of crepe bandage around each ankle. Then he tore four strips of masking tape off a roll and secured the ends of the bandages. Next he pulled on his socks and slipped a pair of shin pads as big as ridge tiles down the front, and wrapped masking tape around the top and bottom of each pad. He took another two lengths of crepe bandage and wrapped one around each thigh and tied them with more tape. Then he took a ribbed brown bottle of white liniment from the line of items and rubbed it into what little flesh remained on view. The old familiar pungent smell, somewhere between mothballs and vinegar, was so strong it made Brian squint and turn away. Then Col stuck his finger into a jar of Vic and pushed the clear jelly up each nostril before smearing Vaseline over his eyebrows. Finally, he pulled on his training shoes and tied identical knots in each lace. Brian was so engrossed, trying hard not to laugh or say anything, that he put both legs into one leg of his shorts.

Duggan instructed everyone to jog around the perimeter of the training ground as a warm up. Col galloped off in front, despite the weight handicap of pads and the restriction of tight bandages. Steve tried to keep up with Alan but ended up walking after three laps, complaining that Alan was cheating by running on the inside lane. Stuart threw his cigarette away and jogged round with Jeff and neither spoke. Malc, with a strapping on his bad knee, jogged round at the back with Brian.

Duggan told everyone to stretch their hamstrings. The drill was to touch your toes then reach for the sky, repeated ten times. Brian struggled. The ground seemed a long way down and only Alan had retained enough flexibility to complete the exercise without bending his knees or groaning.

Stuart seemed to think stretching was something to do with pulling down his tight shirt.

'When are we going to get the ball out, Tommy?'

Eventually Duggan allowed them to play football. For most of the time the game was played at jogging pace with the occasional short burst of optimistic sprinting. Alan had not lost the skill of closing people down and he never gave the ball away. Stuart could still slow the game to his pace and he never broke sweat. Steve was playing from memory and when not under pressure made some lovely weighted cross field passes. Phil tried to control the ball the way he used to do when he scored those wonderful goals, but his timing was poor, and he fell over a couple of times when there was no one anywhere near him. Jeff tried his best, but he lacked confidence. Would he always be seen as the second team goalkeeper? Col decided to play the whole game on the right flank, close to the side netting nearest the car park after Malc told him there was a man leaning on a car in the car park making notes. Malc thought he might be a scout from an over-fifties club.

Steve was the first player to tell his team mates he needed to sit down for a minute and get his breath back, and within a few minutes everyone joined him on the benches and the training session was over.

'Have you got any angina tablets on that chemist's bench, Col?' Phil said. 'I'm knackered.'

Col pretended to search inside his kit bag.

'No, but I've got some Statins and some blood pressure tablets in here somewhere if they're any good to you.'

Steve said, 'If you've got any Viagra tablets in there give Alan a couple.'

Stuart lit a cigarette and took a deep drag.

'How long have we been training, Tommy?'

Duggan looked at his watch.

'Thirty minutes. We're going to have to do a lot better than that if we want to be the best over-fifties side around here.'

The players changed out of their training gear and Brian asked if everybody was going back to the Station for a pint. Phil and Jeff said they were in need of some liquid refreshment after all that exertion. Alan said he'd take Steve back and have a quick half, but then he had to be off.

'Are you coming back, Col?'

'I don't know, Brian. I might do. It depends. I've a few things on. I'll see.'

Everyone stopped talking, slowed their bag packing, deodorant spraying and knee rubbing, and waited for Col to make his mind up. Brian wanted to ask what it depended on, but Col's smile was weak and he wouldn't look at anyone. He was closing up.

Duggan saw the silence as an opportunity. Like picking the pocket of someone laid out on the ground.

'You'd be no good in the trenches. Can't make a simple decision.'

'We didn't rule the empire by dithering,' Pete said, hiding behind Duggen's broad shoulders.

Col took the jibes, his thin smile became even weaker, and finally he said he would skip the pub.

Stuart told Brian he wouldn't be going back to the pub either, because he was taking his girlfriend out for a meal. Steve fastened his watch and made an exaggerated check of the time.

'It's Wednesday. Who are you going out with today?'

'You'll not know her. Her name's Aami. She's from Bradford. I think I'm in love again.'

'You've done well to find a white woman in Bradford.'

'She's not white. She's British-Asian. Her parents are from India. She was born in Bradford.'

Duggan laughed at Stuart.

'The next time we have a training session he'll be wearing a loin cloth.'

Brian sighed and shook his head.

'It's like being back in the nineties. The eighteen nineties.'

On the way out of the ground Col touched Brian's elbow and asked him if he had a minute. They pulled away from the rest of the squad and Col quietly apologised for not going back to the Station with the others. His daughter had suffered a miscarriage last week, he said, and he thought he'd better get back home to be with his wife because she was on her own and having a hard time. Ahead of them, and almost too quiet to hear, Steve asked Stuart about his new girlfriend. In the absence of an audience, his questions were sensitive, there was no joking, and he did everything bar apologise.

8

Brian managed to get away early from the building site in Wakefield where he was doing the roofing work on a new housing estate. He drove straight home, had a quick shower, picked Malc up, and drove to Woodland Park in Clayton village to watch Carers United play Masons FC.

Kick-off was at six-thirty and they arrived ten minutes early. It was still five to twelve according to the bandstand clock. The two sides were warming up at opposite ends of the pitch, Masons FC in red, Carers United in white. Brian and Malc went over to the nearside touch line where Jean had set up her dugout and they stood close enough to shout hello and far enough away not to intrude on her coaching.

None of the white shirts worn by the Carers United team matched. Some had long sleeves, some had short sleeves and one had no sleeves at all. The shorts ranged from grey to blue to black, and the mix of socks could have been donated by the Barbarians rugby team. The players looked ragged compared with the Masons FC players in their uniform red and black kit. Carers United would be feeling one-nil down already in the psychological game.

Harry, the handyman, had just finished marking out the seven-a-side pitch with powdered chalk. He shook the paper sack he had been using to pour the chalk, tied it with orange twine and carried it back to his wheelbarrow close to where Jean was standing. The marked out lines were a little bit wobbly but Brian didn't say anything. He would never criticise the voluntary work Harry did. Harry cared.

The pitch was ready. Corner flags made from yellow dusters stapled to wooden broom handles had been hammered into the hard ground and the white mini goal posts and nets supplied by the away side were in position. The thirty or so Sheffield supporters, mainly women and young girls, in their red and black scarves on the far side of the pitch, outnumbered the home side supporters on the near side by three to one. The three girls and three lads watching from inside the bandstand wore nothing to indicate which team, if any, they supported. The few youths sitting on the swings and the seesaw in the children's play area were too far away to count as spectators. A man strolling by with a brown and white dog on a long lead said good luck to Jean and Harry and their little band of supporters. On the far side of the pitch a figure in camouflage shorts and top rode a mountain bike at walking pace round and round the flower bed.

'Jean takes this coaching very seriously,' Brian said.

'I can tell by the way she's geeing up her players,' Malc said. 'You'd think it was a world cup qualifier.'

'She's like that with her staff at the care home.'

'The good thing for me is there doesn't seem to be any prima donnas among them. That makes a change from men's football. Let's hope they stay like that. Hello. Is that Steve and Alan?' Malc pointed to two figures entering the park from the car park.

Brian waved and their two friends altered course and came over.

Steve never took the time to tune into a group he was joining – he always tried to steer it. He was a comedian and never off duty. Brian had come to the conclusion it was all a cover and deep down Steve was unhappy. You got a sense of that, when you saw how easily he could switch from being the funny guy to someone capable of shutting someone up with a nasty remark. When he was okay, everyone was okay. When he was unhappy, everyone was a target.

'Jeez. There's some tidy young things out there.'

Malc said, 'You're too old for all that, Steve.'

'He wouldn't know what to do if one of those women came across here,' Alan said in his usual soft voice.

'I would if that tall, leggy goalkeeper came over. She's a looker. I'm glad my hormones are in the right place.'

Brian shook his head. He'd had a little private bet with himself on how long it would take Steve to change the tone. This was a near record.

A woman standing next to the Masons FC coach took her red tracksuit off and jogged onto the pitch. She was dressed in black shorts and black top and when she reached the centre circle she blew her whistle. Both sets of players stopped exercising and stretching and Gloria and the opposing team captain jogged over to the referee. They shook hands and the referee tossed a coin. The three heads followed the arc and the referee showed the result to the two captains. Gloria rolled up her sleeves, the biker tattoo on her big pale forearm an intimidating sight, and pointed to the end in front of the bed of begonias.

Both teams appeared to be playing the same system with three defenders, two midfielders and one up front. Both sides held their formation and were not tempted to chase the ball. The tall athletic Kalina, playing in goal for Masons FC, looked unbeatable standing tall between the posts of the seven-a-side nets; whereas Sylvia, at around five foot six, in the Carers United goal looked vulnerable.

There were shouts of encouragement and applause from Jean and Harry and the Carers United supporters, and much louder support from the Masons FC end, especially the screams of excitement from the young girls waving their red and black scarves.

Alan, who had been watching the game with the concentration of a football scout, was impressed with the standard and the level of skill. He picked out Aisha and Helen and a couple of women from Masons FC who he said were intelligent players. At first Steve delivered all the old jokes he used to come out with in his playing days: "Has she got a biscuit tin on her foot?" when a player skewed the ball skywards. "Is somebody injured?" when a player misjudged a ball and kicked it out of play. "I've seen milk turn faster," when a player struggled to get back into position.

By half time Carers United were four nil down. Jean was giving her half time team talk near the centre circle when something nudged Brian's calf. It was the knobbly front wheel of a mountain bike, the same mountain bike he had seen being ridden around the flower bed by the figure in camouflage. Duggan laughed at the suspicious expression on the faces of his former footballing colleagues.

'I didn't know you were a cyclist,' Brian said.

'What a load of shite.'

No one responded. Was he talking about his mountain bike or the game of football? Brian didn't ask; he could see from Duggan's eyes he wasn't in the mood for humour.

'I've just watched the whole of that first half and if that's women's football you can shove it up your arse.'

'You'll not be watching the second half then, Tommy,' Alan said.

'I'm not. I'd rather watch paint dry.' Duggan turned to Brian. 'I've been thinking. If we struggle to get eleven players together from the old Acorn side, why don't we open it up and see if anybody's interested from any of the other teams we used to play against? We could put a right eleven-a-side team together. We'd be able to take on any over-fifties side, anywhere.'

Steve and Alan nodded and said it sounded like a good idea. Malc turned away and stared across the park. Brian stroked his chin.

'I think we'd better have a meeting between everybody involved. We need to discuss how we're going to approach this seven-a-side over-fifties thing.'

Malc took his mobile out.

'Next Wednesday would be good for me.'

'Why wait till then?' Duggan said. 'Leave it with me. I'll contact everybody and set up a meeting this week at the Station.' He spun the crank arm on his bike ready to push off. 'You're serious about playing against this lot? What a waste of time.'

He rode away, laughing and shaking his head. Malc waited until Duggan was too far away to hear.

'And have a pleasant evening yourself.'

Carers United quickly pulled two goals back and narrowly lost four-three. Brian told Jean her side were easily the better team in the second half. Her words of encouragement at half time had done the trick.

Brian and Malc walked back to the car park with Steve and Alan; they talked about football and no one mentioned Duggan. In the confines of his van Brian turned to Malc.

'Bollocks to Duggan. I will organise a seven-a-side match between my dad's care home and a new Acorn team, with or without him.'

9

There were no windows in the meeting room at the Station Inn. The only light was from a fluorescent tube above the rectangular table. There was hardly enough space to pull out the chairs and the wallpaper was scuffed in a rough line where the hard backs had repeatedly banged into the wall. When the door was closed to keep out the loud music and raised voices from the bar area, it was like being inside a sealed shipping container. All six former Acorn players who had shown an interest in getting back together had turned up for the evening meeting; Jeff, Steve, Alan, Col, Stuart and Phil. Brian was sitting next to Malc in front of a flip chart, and directly opposite was Duggan and his ever present taxi man, Pete. When everyone had taken a swig of beer and got used to sitting closer than normal to each other, playfully knocking knees and elbows and complaining about a lack of space, Brian opened the meeting.

'Thanks for coming, lads. And thanks for organising it, Tommy.'

Duggan nodded across the table without smiling as if to say, 'Right you two. Let's see what you've got to say for yourselves.' Duggan was the only one with his arms resting on the table. His elbows were sticking out so much, Pete on his right and Col on his left had to lean away from him and twist their bodies so as not to feel excluded from the meeting. Brian put his arms on the table to claim an equal share of space. When he tried to straighten his legs his feet met Duggan's feet. There was no surrender of territory from Duggan and Brian had to withdraw. It was awkward. There was a force keeping him and Duggan apart. It reminded him of the physics lesson at school when he first tried to get two magnets of the same pole to come together. Impossible.

'The reason we've called this meeting is to make some joint decisions on a couple of things. My lovely assistant here will keep a track on what we agree.'

Malc, who had been playing with a red felt tip pen, snapping the top on and off, stood up and turned over the front blank sheet of the flip chart and revealed the two agenda items.

'Oh no,' Phil said. 'Not another one of the gentleman electrician's famous lists.'

Malc mouthed piss off and Phil replied with two fingers. The friendly exchange allowed everybody, except Duggan who never moved, to fidget and nudge and take another few seconds to settle down.

'Right. First thing. We need to make a decision on whether we want to run a seven-a-side team or an eleven-a-side team. I know you've got some thoughts on this, Tommy.'

Duggan took his elbows off the table and sat back in his chair.

'We should go for an eleven-a-side team. We should be ambitious, never mind pussyfooting around in a seven-a-side league. We don't have to stick to the old Acorn players. We could open it up to one or two of the top teams we used to play against, like Filbert Albion and the Cross Keys. I reckon they'd have one or two ex-players who'd be keen to join us. I've already sounded a few out.

79

We'd easily get eleven players. We'd have a great side. We could take on anybody in any competition anywhere.'

Col was already sold on the idea. Competitions meant medals. Brian envied Col's attitude to football. Col was an average player and he knew it, but he believed in himself and took criticism as a gift. Phil, too, was in favour of an eleven-a-side team in the top tier. He had a dreamy look on his face as though he was watching himself score some wonderful goals at some wonderful grounds again. It was strange. Phil never used to be a bragger. If anything he tended to underplay his achievements. He was a living example of that old saying: 'The older I get the better I was.'

Stuart stayed as cool as ever about the idea and shrugged his broad, square shoulders. Everything he did was cool. Was that because he was such a good looking character and all the women fancied him, even now, despite losing most of his long dark hair and putting on a few inches around his waist? Was the confidence and composure he showed as a footballer partly the result of having the looks of a fashion model? Making him a cool footballer with the ability to dictate the pace of the game? Some sort of respect from the opposition?

Steve on the other hand looked a bit worried that he might not get in the side if top players from other sides were invited. Yes, he was still joking and laughing but you could see in his eyes he wasn't as engaged as usual. Of course Alan had his usual angelic smile on his face. He didn't appear too concerned whichever way it went; eleven-a-side or seven-a-side. He would get in any team and if, for some reason, he wasn't picked he would go for a pleasant three mile run in the woods and enjoy the fresh air.

And Jeff. What was he thinking? He wouldn't look at Brian. He knew how much it meant to him to put together a seven-a-side team and play against the women care workers from Woodland House. Had he been nobbled by Duggan? You'd think he would have some sympathy for the care workers who were looking after their dad. But then you would think he would have found the courage to visit the home by now.

Pete said, 'Why don't we put it to a vote?'

Four hands went up straightaway in favour of Duggan's proposal. Slowly, one after another, four more hands went up. Brian glared at Jeff; it was a good job his brother's head was down. Only Brian and Malc voted for a seven-a-side team. Malc wrote the result on the flip chart.

'So on to the second item. Do we want to take up the challenge thrown down by the Woodland House women's seven-a-side team that I mentioned at the reunion?'

There were a few moans and a few smiles of doubt. Duggan looked left then right with a manufactured confused look on his face.

'I thought we'd already agreed we were going for an eleven-a-side team. Do we want to be taken seriously or what? Forget playing seven-a-side against a bunch of tarts. Everybody'll think we're a set of tossers.' Duggan's finger swept around the table left to right in an arc. 'This is the core of the new Acorn over-fifties eleven-a-side team. Do you want to be laughed at? Or do you want to be the best?'

He sat back, arms folded, job done. Pete whispered well done and he may even have patted Duggan's knee under the table. Brian's aim had simply been to have a reunion and put a friendly seven-a-side team together to play against Jean's care workers in Woodland Park. Nothing serious. Something to help the women improve their game. Something to show his appreciation of the work the care home was doing for his dad and the other residents. Something to show he cared.

'Before we take a vote, me and Malc would just like to make a few points.' Brian stood up and Malc flipped over to a new blank sheet. 'There are some advantages in playing a seven-a-side game against the Carers United team. For a start, as far as me and Malc know, it would be the first football match in Brodworth between an over-fifties men's side and a team of young women care workers from a local care home.'

'Or maybe the first time in Yorkshire,' Malc said. 'We'd be making history.'

'Can you imagine the press coverage the match would get? The all-male New Acorn versus the all-female Carers United. We'd be on the front page *and* the back page of the Brodworth Chronicle.'

'And maybe even the Yorkshire Post.'

'We'd get loads turning up to watch us. All those women supporters fainting at the sight of Stuart in his shorts.'

'Maybe hundreds.'

'Somebody might even make a video of the game.'

'And if it went viral...can you imagine?'

'And we could have a special trophy made just for that contest. It could be an annual challenge.'

There was murmuring and nudging and head wobbling. Brian winked at Malc. Duggan's face glowed red. The room door half opened, banging into the back of Pete's chair. Music and voices from the bar came in, and a man with a bushy beard and thick glasses, pewter tankard in hand, asked if this was the Labour Party meeting.

'Sorry, mate,' Brian said. 'You've got the wrong room.'

'Are you sure? I thought we'd booked it from seven o'clock.'

Duggan swung round.

'Piss off.'

The man's head shrunk into his shoulders and he backed out of the room and closed the door quietly. No one said anything. Duggan switched his stare to the flip chart. Brian smoothed the paper flat with the palm of his hand.

'I propose we take up the challenge thrown down to us by the seven-a-side women's team from Woodland House. Unless, that is, we're too frightened to play against a bunch of tarts.'

10

It was cinema matinee time at Woodland House, a first for Brian, and he was early. Some of the relatives had been to a matinee at the home before. You'll love it they told Brian. Residents, no matter how agitated, behaved like angels as soon as the film began, they said. Earlier that afternoon, Brian had helped Harry, and a couple of permanent staff, move the comfy chairs in the lounge downstairs into a large semi-circle facing the big new TV screen. Harry had installed the TV the day before and it was working fine. He told Brian it had been bought with the proceeds of last year's annual summer charity event held in Woodland Park, where local businesses and individuals donated goods for the home to sell. Under the supervision of Jean and Harry, members of staff and relatives of residents had erected stalls, and brought boxes of goods from the care home to the park. They helped put up the bouncy castle, loaned by Mary's grandson who worked in the leisure industry, and cleared up afterwards. It had been a very enjoyable day, raising hundreds of pounds, matched by Jon Hunt, the owner of Woodland House.

Now, an hour before the film was due to begin, Brian and Jean were outside the kitchen discussing the match between Carers United and Masons FC over a cup of tea. He told Jean how much he had enjoyed the game and Jean said she had learned a few lessons and hoped for a better result in the return match at Masons FC's ground.

'Good news about the new Acorn side.' Brian said. 'We had a meeting the other day and agreed to put together a seven-a-side team and take you up on your challenge.'

'That's fantastic,' Jean said, and she held up her cup and they said cheers. 'I knew you'd do it. All we need to do now is organise the where and when. Do you want me to call a meeting?'

'Fine. Me and Malc can represent the new Acorn, although keeping Tommy Duggan out of it could be a problem. He likes to be in charge. You met him the other day in the beer garden. He was the one who threw the ball over the wall.'

'Invite him as well. Keep him on side.'

'Good move. We'll work round you. I know you'll need to sort out your staff shift patterns. We don't want you fielding a weakened side. No excuses.'

'We'll be alright as long as Aisha gets her form back. She's dipped a bit in training lately.'

'It happened to me a few times when I was playing. Even professionals lose their form.'

'We'll see.'

'Me and Malc's got some ideas about promoting the match if that's something you want to do.'

'Definitely. I'm up for anything that'll raise money for the care home and give my lasses a chance to come together and play a game of football.'

Half an hour later, in the big lounge downstairs, the video was in its slot, the new TV was on and 'The Wizard of Oz' was on pause on the screen. Nearly all of the residents, twenty five in total from both floors, were in their cushioned seats or parked in their wheelchairs waiting for the show to begin. Mary and a resident from downstairs were warming up, merrily waltzing with

Mahsa, the home's hairdresser, and Aisha as though they were on the dance floor of a cruise ship. Brian was sitting with his dad and Arthur on hard backed chairs, drinking at the temporary bar, as realistic as any pub with its cans of beer, cartons of wine, fruit juices and bowls of crisps. Gloria, motorbike tattoo on show, had volunteered to be the bar woman for the evening with the added responsibility of monitoring the drinks consumed. Brian's dad was allowed two cans of beer, Arthur was allowed one, and those residents with less mobility were allowed drinks according to their condition. The good news was everybody could eat as much ice cream as they liked. Gloria kept an eye on everyone. She was a good host. It was a disciplined regime delivered in a relax way. Maybe the tattoo helped.

Brian had insisted on paying for his dad's drinks out of his own pocket, even though there was eleven pounds fifty remaining in his dad's weekly allowance to cover the cost. The information pack Brian received from the local authority detailing how the weekly allowance was worked out was a bit of a shock, both in the paltry sums involved and the slightly patronising tone. A government set weekly personal expenses allowance of thirty pounds fifteen pence was set aside from the resident's income to make sure residents still had some money for everyday essentials and personal items. This applied even where the resident's income was insufficient to meet their care costs. The local authority had discretion to increase the amount based on an individual's needs. The personal expenses allowance belonged to the resident and it could be spent on whatever the resident liked. The benefit claimant tone confirmed what Brian had been denying to himself for months; his dad was no longer an independent person. He was part of an institution.

Brian clicked plastic glasses with his dad and Arthur.

'It's not a bad club this, is it Dad.'

'It's okay.'

'What do you reckon to the beer, Arthur?'

Arthur was back to his old self, red cheeks and bright blue eyes. He put his drink down and patted his safety helmet.

'It's good stuff.'

'Are you looking forward to the film, you two?'

Both smiled back.

'They're putting the Wizard of Oz on. Remember it, Dad? Judy Garland. Yellow Brick Road.'

'Yellow Brick Road.'

Kalina, as activities coordinator, was in overall charge of the matinee. It was her first time and Jean had volunteered to work unpaid that afternoon to support her. They were standing next to Brian drinking tea and chatting, Jean instructing Kalina on the rules and regulations for the event.

'Just make sure everybody's back in their seats by half past four so you can serve the ice cream and start the film on time. Aisha will close the blinds and dim the lights. Gloria will collect all the plastic beakers and cups and put them out of the way behind the bar. Then they'll give you a hand to serve the ice cream.'

'Okay. I think I have got that.'

'Do you know how to work the video?'

'Yes. I have a video at home.'

'Have you seen 'The Wizard of Oz'? It's brilliant.'

'Many times. It is a popular film in Poland. Judy Garland is memorable.'

Kalina checked her watch. 'I will get everybody in their seats now.' She walked over to the TV and clapped her hands.

Mahsa and Aisha thanked Mary and her friend for the dance and led them back to their seats. Gloria gave the bar top a quick wipe and stepped out from behind the counter.

'Come on, Joe. Come on, Arthur. Time to watch the film. You don't want to miss the start. And if you're not in your seats in two minutes, there'll be no ice cream left for you.'

Joe and Arthur's eyes lit up like excited children and Gloria led them step by step to their seats. Brian couldn't control the smile on his face and he shook his head in admiration. How easily the care workers persuaded the residents to willingly follow instructions. No resistance. No drama. He had tried to copy their technique but it almost always ended in failure. All the staff in the home, from the manager, to the kitchen ladies, to Mahsa, the hairdresser, had the magic. He couldn't unlock the code. It must be in the tone of their voice. Or perhaps the way they made eye contact. Or was it the way they treated the residents like adults but with child-like needs? That could be it.

Kalina managed to get everyone settled into their comfy chairs and eating ice cream, or being helped to eat ice cream, out of little white cardboard tubs with little flat wooden spoons. At quarter to five sharp, the blinds were closed, the lights were dimmed, the room fell silent, and the film began.

Brian and Jean stayed at the bar, a yard apart, their chairs facing the screen. Jean leaned sideways, eyes fixed on the film.

'Peace at last.'

Brian waited a couple of seconds then leaned towards Jean, his eyes also fixed on the film.

'They look like little kids at the Odeon on a Saturday morning, only better behaved. I'm waiting for somebody to throw their ice cream carton at the screen.'

'Or kick it up in the air and smash the light fitting.'

'Oh no,' Brian said. 'Not again.'

His laugh was a bit too loud. Kalina looked up from her seat near the front and Brian covered his mouth.

Dorothy was in the farmyard with Toto, singing 'Somewhere over the Rainbow.' Brian's dad and his fellow residents were spellbound by the movement of colour across the big screen, and the wonderful sounds coming to life around them. Brian had forgotten how sentimental the film was. But it was still magical. Just wait until Dorothy is dancing down the yellow brick road with the Tin Man and the Scarecrow and the Cowardly Lion.

He carefully lifted his chair clear of the floor and moved it closer to Jean, not too close.

'How's my dad been lately, Jean?'

'He's been fine, Brian. Absolutely fine. You've nothing to worry about there. He's settled in really well. It can take some people a while to get used to their new home. Everybody's different, but your dad's settled in fine.'

'That's comforting to know. I tried my best to keep him in his own home but it was impossible. I knew it was getting bad when he didn't know how to sign my Christmas card last year. He tried, the old lad. He really tried. You could see the concentration on his face. He was staring at the card, the way he used to do when he was working through his racing book with his red biro trying to find a winner.'

'It's hard.'

'It got while he couldn't even put his jacket on and I had to fasten the zip up for him. It would have been funny if it hadn't been so sad. I think that's when he realised there was something not right.'

Whenever Brian glanced at Jean, testing her reaction, checking if she was secretly tutting at him for telling her things she must have heard a thousand times from relatives, things he'd not told anyone else, she was looking over the heads of the silent audience towards the screen.

'He started going walkabout. Me and the young carer lass who used to visit tried to lock him in but he had a swing at both of us. We even fitted an alarm to the front door but he managed to find a way round it. One of the neighbours found him one day wandering up the road in his pyjamas at six o'clock in the morning. He said he was going to the pit.'

'It happens, Brian.'

'It wouldn't have been so bad if he'd thought he was going on holiday.' Brian laughed quietly. It was gallows humour. He wanted to lighten the conversation. He was also probing Jean's character, her humour, trying to find some common ground. She smiled and nodded and her eyes crinkled at the corners. A connection. 'I couldn't ask him to move in with me, not with me working every day. He'd have gone bananas in no time.'

'Everybody feels guilty when they get to the stage of putting their loved one into a care home. It's normal. It's okay.'

The Cowardly Lion started to sing and Brian's dad looked mesmerized. Brian's throat tightened and he wanted to hold Jean's hand. Just for comfort, nothing else.

'Thanks for that, Jean.'

'It's okay. I was looking through my files and I see your dad's birthday's coming up soon.'

Brian sat back in his chair and gave himself ten out of ten for not letting tears well up.

'It is.'

'We'll have to organise a party for him.'

'That would be great. Let me know if there's anything you want me to do, or anything I need to buy, and I'll sort it out with you. I'm hoping our Jeff might finally decide to visit, seeing as it's my dad's birthday.'

The film was almost over. You could tell it was nearing the end even if you'd never seen the film before. The music had changed and the mood had moved from trepidation to optimism. Dorothy was there, centre stage in her silver shoes, Toto under her arm; Scarecrow, Tin Man and Cowardly Lion gathered around, each looking at the little girl with love and hope for a safe return home – it was an enchanting scene. Were the spellbound residents aware the film was coming to an end? Would they feel any different tonight as the carers tucked them in and turned the lights out? He had read somewhere that the heart doesn't get dementia. It was a lovely thought. But was it just another Hollywood ending?

The light and movement of the final few scenes flickered across Jean's face. There was a hint of softness in her mouth, as soft as Susan's, something he hadn't noticed before. He was a young man again, on the back row of the cinema, Susan at his side, a carefree, endless future in front of him. He swallowed hard. He was out of practice but the timing felt right.

'Do you fancy going out for a drink one night next week?'

Jean turned her head slowly and looked into his eyes. Had he got it wrong? Was she about to laugh at him?

'Next week?' she said. 'I didn't know you cared.'

11

Brian threw his van keys to Jeff, and left him pacing up and down the care home car park while he signed in. He had tried yet again, despite telling himself it was futile, to get Jeff to visit their dad and this time he'd had a bit of success. His brother said he would hang around the car park, and if he could pluck up the courage to go into the home, he would give Brian a call on his mobile and ask him to meet him at reception and take him up.

Brian had to pass the hairdresser's room on the way to the lift and the door was open. His dad was sitting on a straight backed chair with a white sheet around his shoulders. Mahsa was enjoying cutting his dad's hair as much as his dad was enjoying having it cut. Jean told Brian all the residents loved and responded to the human touch, such as the simple act of having their scalp massaged. Residents looked forward to the experience, she said. And we take our time with them.

'They look after you in here, Dad, don't they. Not only do you get food and lodgings but you get your hair trimmed by a lovely young woman. Morning Mahsa.'

Mahsa took the compliment with an exaggerated flick of her long straight black hair.

'Good morning, Brian. We're having a lovely time, aren't we Joe.'

There was no need for a reply, the smile said it all. His dad looked like a Mohican with his grey hair combed high ready for the scissors to start snipping. The shapeless, motionless white sheet beneath the exposed head made his dad look helpless and childlike. How many times had a young Brian and Jeff sat immobile on the kitchen chair at home, a white sheet around their shoulders, having their hair cut by their dad? His hands shaped by digging coal, digging roads, and carpet fitting, and yet capable of an action as delicate as that which Mahsa's long slender fingers were doing right now.

'You've had your bath as well this morning, haven't you Joe.'

'Ah. That's why you're smiling, Dad. I know I keep saying it Mahsa, but you're all doing a wonderful job at this place.'

'I'll be finished in half an hour then you can have your new dad back.'

'I'll go and see how Arthur and Mary and the others are getting on. See you in a bit, Dad.'

When Brian stepped out of the lift, Jean was at her desk in a corner of the dining area next to the lounge writing something in her red ring binder. She looked up, took her glasses off and rubbed her eyes.

'Your dad's downstairs having his hair cut.'

'I've just seen him. He looks ten years younger. Mahsa's great with him. You all are.'

Jean dropped her pen onto the desk, leaned back in her chair and rolled her shoulders.

'We're supposed to have gone digital but there's more paperwork now than there's ever been.'

As a self-employed joiner working on his own he found paperwork a bind. Susan used to do the books. She was good at it.

'Is it all reports and other very important things?'

'Health and safety, medication reports, updating regulations, Care Quality Commission inspection. You name it. But I'm not complaining – it's all essential stuff. I'm studying for my senior care worker qualification. It's all good experience. Good on the job training.'

Jean put her glasses back on then took them off again when Brian asked how her seven-a-side team were coming on.

'We're looking good, although I'm still a bit concerned about Aisha. She's the lynchpin, and Kalina's made a huge difference. Not just her goalkeeping prowess but her energy. She's amazing, that lass. She's holding down three jobs.'

'Our team's coming on. Our Jeff, my brother, is in goal. He's looking well in training.'

'Is that your Jeff who I see sitting in your van sometimes, or walking round the car park looking lost?'

'That's him.'

'I don't think I've ever seen him visiting your dad. Have you told him we don't bite?'

'He keeps saying he wants to visit, and I keep picking him up. He got as far as the toilets the other day when those two from Lost Harmonies were here. But he backed out. I wouldn't mind, but I only live five minutes away. It's a twenty mile round trip by the time I've picked him up and dropped him off again. But he doesn't drive. I know he's my brother, but I'm not his keeper.'

'Buses run through Clayton every half hour. We get a bit spaced out in this village now and again, but we're not on the moon.'

'He'll never come in. It's a long story and it goes back a long way. I'm not even sure how it all started. He might tell me one day, if he ever finds the courage to visit my dad. He's outside now thinking about it. Again. He says he'll give me a ring if he decides to come up. But he's not got the bottle. He'll not visit.'

Brian's mobile rang and he pulled the Nokia out of his back pocket.

'Hang on. I might have to eat my words.'

He turned away from Jean to answer. His voice soon dropped.

'Aye, okay, Jeff. Don't worry about it. I'll be about half an hour.'

'I take it your brother's not coming.'

'Is he hell. I told you.'

'Burner phone?'

Brian's Nokia mobile seemed to get stubbier and smaller each time he used it.

'Yeah. I've some dodgy business going on.'

'Don't tell my lad. He's easily tempted.'

Brian knew about her son's tangles with the law. She'd casually mentioned it to him one day, very early on, maybe the first month his dad came to the home. But she didn't say what kind of trouble he'd been in. She never mentioned a partner or any other children. Maybe she'd brought the lad up on her own. Imagine, doing a full time job at the care home six days a week then going home and having to sort out your lad's problems. Sometimes Brian was glad he and Susan never had children.

The two-tone sound of a vacuum cleaner being pushed and pulled a few yards round the corner from Jean's desk grew louder.

Here she comes,' Jean said. 'Our little dynamo.'

The front end of the machine appeared and disappeared then Aisha came into view. When she saw Jean and Brian she switched the vacuum off.

'I'm sorry, Jean. I did not know you were busy.'

'We were just talking about you. I was telling Brian how important you are to the football team.'

Aisha turned away and yanked the flex without answering. It was a strange response. Jean was as puzzled as Brian. She put her finger to her lips and stood up from her desk.

'Unplug the vac, Aisha. Come and have a cup of tea in the kitchen where it's quiet.'

Jean put her arm around Aisha and led her through to the kitchen at the far end of the empty dining room. They left the door open and Brian tried to listen in to what was being said but all he could hear were voices from the TV in the lounge next door. Should he shout goodbye and leave quietly? After all, it was none of his business. But Aisha looked upset, and so did Jean. If there was anything he could do...

He put his head around the kitchen door. The two women were sitting on a wooden bench in between the refrigerator and the sink. Jean was stroking Aisha's back.

Brian said, 'Is everything alright?'

There was no one else in the room. The kitchen seemed to be on pause. Everything was turned off and silent; the hob and the oven, the dishwasher at the side of the waste bin, the radio on the windowsill, even the clock on the wall above the microwave made no sound. Aisha looked up, tears running down her cheeks, and said everything was okay. Jean shook her head at Brian. He held onto the door for support, neither in nor out.

'Can I do anything?'

'Aisha's a bit upset aren't you, love.'

'I am feeling vulnerable and frightened.'

'Come in, Brian.'

Aisha blew her nose and smiled a thank you to Jean.

The bench was only big enough for two and Brian crouched down in front of them. On the worktop at the side of Jean there was a bowl of white, peeled potatoes submerged in cold water. In the sink a dishcloth had been folded over the tap spout. There was a faint smell of drains and bleach.

'I am sorry to be a burden, Jean. I do not want to cause any trouble.'

'It's no trouble, you daft thing.'

The metal appliances and hard tiled floor caused a little echo, making their words sharper than when in the carpeted rooms and corridor.

'Next door to the house where I live, I have made a friend who I am very worried about. She is from India. She is a home care worker. She told me she paid thousands of pounds to get sponsorship and to obtain a visa to work in the care sector. I only paid a few hundred pounds for my sponsorship.'

'That's all it should cost,' Jean said.

'They told her the money was to cover travel to the UK and accommodation. She thought she was paying legitimate fees because the agent was based in the UK but now she knows she was deceived.'

Jean nodded and listened as though neither shocked nor surprised, and she continued to stroke Aisha's back. Brian, clumsy and not sure why he was there, offered his opinion.

'They want shopping, the bastards.'

'When she arrived in the UK everything seemed okay at first. She was employed by a home care provider straightaway and they found her accommodation – the house next to where I live. The flat is cramped and dark but she thought that was normal. She was happy and relieved. But the care provider only gave her a few hours of work each week. After a few weeks they stopped paying her wages saying the local authority was to blame.'

'The local authority aren't brilliant,' Jean said, 'but they're not that bad.'

'After just three months she was told her job had been terminated. She was devastated. She told me she was suicidal. They owe her money for all the weeks they have not paid her, and she has used all her savings to pay for her sponsorship. She had no choice but to use the foodbank.'

'They sound like a set of crooks to me,' Brian said. 'Taking advantage of vulnerable people, the swines. It's exploitation. Why doesn't your friend report them to the police?'

'Or the social services?' Jean said.

'They have kept her passport. If she goes to the police or the social services, the home care provider has threatened to report her for the money they say she owes them. They have allowed her to stay in her flat but she is running up a big debt. She says the flat is unhealthy. It is just a tiny room that she shares with six other women. If she does not find another job within six months she could be deported back to India. She does not know what to do. She is terrified.'

Jean held Aisha's hand.

'I make no wonder you're feeling so scared and vulnerable. I'd be the same if it was happening to one of my friends.'

'I am very scared for her. I am frightened now that I know what her employer may do to her. She sometimes comes out of the house and we talk in the back garden.

But the landlord is always watching. She is my only friend outside of work. I have no family here. I am on my own.'

'You're not on your own, Aisha. You're part of our family here at Woodland House and we'll always look after you.'

Aisha began to cry and smile at the same time. Brian's knees were aching. The second hand on the clock above the microwave moved smoothly around the clock face. Jeff would be wondering where he was. He stood up and rubbed the outside of his knees in a slow circular motion.

'Did you say your friend lives next door to you?'

'We live on Racecommon Road in Brodworth, near the town centre. My flat is at number fifty seven and my friend's flat is at number fifty five.'

'I know Racecommon Road. I've fitted a few dormers in that area over the years. I might have a ride up there sometime. Do a bit of sales work. See if anybody wants a dormer putting in.'

Jean stopped stroking Aisha's hand.

'Be careful, Brian. They sound like dangerous people.'

'Yes. Please be careful. They are criminals.'

'Don't worry about me. You look after my dad; I'll look after you.'

12

The back gardens of the houses on Racecommon Road and Sheffield Road faced each other, divided by a narrow footpath running the full length of the two terraces. Brian's old friend, Steve had lived at the bottom end of Sheffield Road for years. There was a good chance he would have some knowledge of the comings and goings at number fifty five Racecommon Road.

'Come on in, Brian. What brings you to the back streets of India?'

Steve led Brian into the kitchen. He was in the middle of doing his accounts by the look of the amount of paperwork scattered across the table. Steve moved a pile of letters and receipts off one of the dining chairs and Brian sat down.

'You know the other day when we had that reunion...'

'Yes. It was a good do. I enjoyed it. It was great to catch up with all the old players together under one roof.'

'It was. You said Racecommon Road was being overrun by migrants.'

'It is. They're taking over the whole street. I can see them over the back gardens. You see new black faces up and down that street every day. Mind you, they could all be the same faces; it's hard to tell them apart. And there's east Europeans. I tell you, we'll be living in a foreign country before long if they don't put an end to all this immigration. England as we know it will be a thing of the past.'

Brian smiled and nodded and tried not to get into an argument. His old friend had long ago stopped listening to any point of view that differed from his own. Steve would say Brian was as bad and maybe he was. He had learned to laugh at or ignore Steve's rants. Otherwise they could easily fall out. Their friendship started when they were in their late teens which to Brian, and he hoped to Steve, meant they were bound by loyalty, trust and a shared history. But when it came to what it meant to be British they were miles apart.

'I know somebody who lives in a flat on Racecommon Road. She was telling me about a friend of hers, an Indian woman, who lives next door. She's a bit worried about her.'

'I'd be a bit worried as well if an Indian lived next door to me.'

'No. Listen, Steve. This is serious. Do you ever see or hear of anything dodgy going on in the flats over there?'

'Every day. There's always somebody screaming or shouting. Flash cars with black windows you can't see through pulling up. Big black guys getting in and out. Scooters racing up and down. It'll be drugs, I can guarantee you that. I keep well away.'

'I don't get into the town centre much these days. Have many of the houses on Racecommon Road been converted into flats? It used to be a posh part of Brodworth.'

'So did Sheffield Road. But the area's sinking. We'd get out if we could afford to move.'

'I've converted a few lofts in this area over the years. People were keen to spend money on their houses at one time. Do them up.'

'Not now. Nobody's got any money. Youngsters don't want to work anymore. I had a lad come to me the other month, supposedly to learn a trade. Only lasted a week.

He couldn't get out of bed on a morning. Bone idle, and he's typical.'

'Towns like Brodworth never recovered from the pits closing down. Thirty odd years of neglect. What are the prospects for youngsters these days? You can hardly blame them for feeling hopeless.'

'They'll not find hope lounging around in bed all day long.'

Steve looked out of the kitchen window. His jaw had tightened. The temperature was rising and it wasn't from the sunshine hitting the untidy pile of white papers on the table. It was time to go before another thin layer of friendship peeled away.

Brian left Steve to finish his accounts and drove slowly along Racecommon Road towards number fifty five. He had been in a good mood prior to calling on his old friend. His regular Saturday morning visit to see his dad had been an uplifting start to the day. His dad had been awake all the time and when Brian asked him what he had been up to, he said he had been out for a walk to the shop that morning for his paper. Jean and the other carers told him to go with whatever his dad said and enjoy the moment. His good mood had started to fade at Steve's and now it disappeared altogether as he approached Aisha's neighbour.

The Victorian terraced houses on either side of the road were stone fronted with big bay windows, grey slate roofs and short front gardens three strides deep. There was an arched alleyway every fifty yards or so giving access to the rear. It was top quality housing in its day. Some of the properties were well looked after with good curtains up at the windows and cared for shrubs in the front garden. Others, a creeping minority as Steve had remarked, had been converted into flats, confirmed by the number of extra gas and electricity meter boxes installed in the external walls. There were dozens more than when he last worked in the street a year or two ago. And dozens more wheelie bins in the alleyways and front gardens, each bin with its identifying flat number crudely painted on the side in white gloss. On a few where the paint had run, it looked as though the bins had been crying. It must have been the mood he was in.

He drove slowly past number fifty five. There was no dormer, just a small skylight no bigger than a manhole cover half way up the slate roof. There were cheap bamboo roller blinds behind the two upstairs windows and the big bay window downstairs. All the blinds were fully down, which was a bit strange considering the house faced north and would get little sun for most of the day. A supermarket trolley lay on its side in the front garden and an old mattress had been dumped on the path to the door. The two abandoned items were the only signs that somebody might be living there.

In contrast, at Aisha's house next door, the curtains were open, the windows were clean, and the wheelie bins with their evenly spaced, matching self-adhesive numbers, were parked in a neat line.

Brian drove another fifty yards, parked up and took a handful of his business cards and his notepad from the shelf under the dashboard. It was quiet and there were a lot of windows looking onto the road. Any prying eyes would see the bright yellow sign on his blue van advertising his roof and loft conversion specialism, hardly the transport of a burglar. He knocked on the door of a couple of houses opposite Aisha's. When no one answered, he stood in the middle of the road and looked up at the roofs, pretending to make notes in his notebook before pushing a business card through the letter boxes.

He walked around the dumped mattress outside number fifty five and knocked on the front door. The voices and music coming from what sounded like a TV in the front room continued. There were deep scratches in the red paintwork below the letter box as though a big dog had been trying to get into the house. Above the door, a rough sawn sheet of plywood had been nailed over the transom window. Brian stood on the top step and knocked a second time, louder and longer; a policeman's knock, as his mother used to say. The TV went quiet this time. He waited, expecting to see a finger spread the bamboo blinds. When the blinds remained still and no one came to the door he knocked a third time. A bolt slid across the top of the door followed by another bolt lower down. A lock turned. The door opened an inch. A human eye stared out of the narrow dark opening. Brian smiled and tried to sound bright and happy.

'Morning. I'm just going round the area looking to see if anybody's interested in having a loft conversion or maybe a dormer installed in their attic to make it more usable. I'm a joiner. I've fitted a few on this street over the years.'

The door opened another inch and now two eyes in a shaved head stared at him. Daylight lit up the man's white scalp, making it stand out against the narrow strip of dark hallway. It was difficult to pick out any shape or movement beyond the head.

'I can see there's a skylight in the roof. Is there a flat up there? Are you the landlord by any chance? I was wondering if you might be interested in a quote for a full loft conversion. It'll not take two minutes. No obligation.'

The man yanked the door wide open and pretended to scream into Brian's face. He was barefoot and in his underpants. Brian stepped back, almost tripping over the dumped mattress.

'Bloody hell, Spike. I didn't know you lived here.'

Spike looked up the road to where Brian had parked his van.

'Who said I lived here, matey? I'm just passing through like a hungry rat, keeping an eye on things, watching out for those green men from Mars with their chocolate goodies.'

'I wish I knew what you were on about, Spike. I'll learn the code one day. Are you the landlord?'

Spike stared into Brian's eyes as though daring him to say another word. Or maybe he had his sensible head on and was about to start serenading him.

'I might be. I might not be. And if I am, what's it got to do with you?'

'Whoa, Spike. Take it easy, mate. As I said, I'm looking round the area for work. I've knocked on just about every door on this street. It's a bit quiet at the moment in the building trade.'

'Not interested.'

Spike sat down on the low brick boundary wall separating his and next door's front garden. He crossed his legs which were tanned apart from a narrow strip of white flesh a few inches below his underpants, and smiled at Brian. Had he calmed down? When Brian was captain of the Acorn, he never knew how to handle Spike. He could be brilliant in the first half of a game; skilful, clever, reliable. Then in the second half he could easily turn into a rugby player, felling opponents with waist high tackles. Players would cringe and shake their heads and Brian

106

would have a quiet word with the manager and get him taken off.

Now Brian stood on the pavement outside the house and looked up at the skylight in the roof.

'A dormer would give you a lot more room in the attic. More tenants. More money.'

'Have you got grass in your ears? I said I'm not interested.'

The bamboo blinds at one of the upstairs windows lifted a few inches and three women's faces appeared against the glass. Each had dark brown skin and black hair and they looked down on Brian without smiling.

'Are those women up there okay, Spike? They look as though they're in a bit of distress.'

'You're asking a lot of questions for a joiner. Be wary of woodworm.'

They both turned round at the sound of a scooter racing into view around the corner at the bottom of the street, sparks flying as the two-wheeled machine's runner board scraped the tarmac. It came to a stop outside the alleyway a few yards below number fifty five and the rider and pillion jumped off. Their faces were hidden behind the big chin guards and dark visors of their black and white helmets but they had the swagger of young lads. As they came strutting towards Brian, a long white saloon car, its driver and any passengers concealed from view behind tinted windows, appeared around the same corner and screeched to a stop at the side of Brian. The driver, dark skinned, sunglasses, gold rings like knuckle dusters, stepped out of the vehicle. His tight white suit took on the shape of his bulging shoulders, arms and thighs. He looked as though he was about to shed his outer skin and move up a size.

'Spike,' the big driver said. 'Put a decent pair of pants on when I'm visiting my children. Don't I pay you enough?'

Spike slowly got off the wall, wiped the dust off his hands down the back of his pants, and stared at Brian.

'I'm going inside for a piss. If you know what's good for you, you'll not be here when I come back out.'

Spike stood to one side to let the driver and the two helmeted scooter riders into the house. He followed them in and banged the door shut. Brian put his business cards and notebook in his pocket. As he walked back to his van, the upstairs blinds at number fifty five slowly closed.

13

Jean was standing at the worktop in front of her kitchen window making notes in her notebook, and scrolling through the staffing rota on her mobile phone. The smell of fried bacon lingered in the air, and the suds from the two plates, cups and cutlery she had just washed were slowly draining into the sink. The breeze pushing the low clouds across the sky meant the clothes she had pegged out on the line half an hour ago while Nathan was in bed, would be dry by the time she came home from work at midday to check the post.

Nathan was up at last, sitting at the kitchen table, texting someone on his mobile.

'What time are you seeing Chloe?' Jean said. She didn't look up from her phone.

'Ten o'clock.'

'You'd better be getting a move on then or you'll miss your bus.'

'She'll wait.'

'She'll not wait for ever if she's any sense.'

Nathan stood up and slipped his phone into the back pocket of his jeans.

'I was going to bring Chloe and Summer back here for their dinner tomorrow, Mam. I could fetch us all some fish and chips.'

'Have they started giving them away for free now?'

'What do you mean?'

109

'Well you've no money to pay for them. And I'm certainly not buying them for you again.'

Nathan crept up behind his mother, put his arm around her shoulders and kissed the top of her head.

'Oh go on, Mam. I'll cut the back lawn for you.'

Jean dropped her mobile onto her notebook.

'You don't know you're born, Nathan. You live here rent free, you've got your own bedroom, you get your breakfast served up for you, you get all your clothes washed and ironed. What a life. And I hope you're not thinking of inviting Chloe and Summer to stay overnight this weekend again. I can't keep on looking after them as well as looking after you.'

'Am I hell.' Nathan opened the back door and turned round. 'Just the odd weekend now and then.'

'It's time you found yourself a job. I'm serious, Nathan.'

Jean had to raise her voice because Nathan had stepped outside and she couldn't tell if he was listening. He put his head back round the door.

'I'm trying, Mam. You know I am. But I've more chance of finding buried treasure in Woodland Park than I have of finding a job. See you tonight. Love you.'

Jean shook her head and refused to smile as Nathan walked past the window blowing extravagant kisses at her. Nathan had the same profile as his dad – the man they didn't talk about. Thick black hair, strong jaw, straight back. It was like seeing her ex again, setting off to work when they were first married, the future looking wonderful. That was before he went off the rails after losing his job. Boozing and womanizing. Hitting her and then crying like a baby straight after, saying he was sorry and asking her to forgive him. Then in no time just hitting her. Was that why Nathan had gone off the rails after leaving school? Getting himself in the wrong crowd and ending up in remand? Would it have been different if her ex had still been around, still loving and caring like he was when Nathan was born? Somebody there to set a good example as a father. Somebody Nathan wouldn't answer back. When her ex used to shout upstairs and tell him his breakfast was ready, Nathan would get up straightaway knowing there wouldn't be a second shout. Not like her. She was too caring to let her son be late. Too soft her ex used to say. She would have to shout three or four times before Nathan finally got up. And then he would walk past the window blowing kisses at her on his way to school. Maybe she would find the courage to tell Brian all of this tonight on their date. Maybe not.

14

The walk from his house past the street leading to Woodland House and onto the Miners Arms was steeper than Brian remembered and he was out of breath. It must be nerves. His reflection in the pub door confirmed the wind and sweat had messed up his hair. He tried to reshape his fringe without being noticed, checked his pulse and flies, took a deep breath, and walked into the busy dining room.

Jean was sitting at a table by the window. Red hair like a beacon and she waved and he went over. She was wearing a black dress, not too low cut, and a silver necklace. Her hands were wrapped around her wine glass.

'Have you been here long?' Brian said, and he sat down and rubbed his aching knees. 'It took me longer to walk up that hill than I anticipated. My legs are still as stiff as hell from training the other day.'

'Half an hour. This is my third glass of wine.'

Jean's eyes told Brian she was having him on and his eyes told her he knew.

'I'd better go and get myself three pints then and catch up with you.'

Jean sipped her wine, trying to hide a smile, and when she looked at Brian over her wine glass her eyes sparkled.

'I've only just got my breath back,' she said. 'I had to stay on an extra hour at Woodland House. I jumped in the shower, got changed, and then dashed straight over here. I was panicking. I thought I was going to be late.'

'I'm glad it's not just me. I'm a novice at this dating game.'

'Me too.'

Brian stood up and put his hand in his pocket.

'Are you ready for another drink?'

'A white wine please. And I'm ready to order some food when you are.'

He brought back a wine and a pint and they both chose a pizza from the menu on the table. Jean went for the spicy meat one. Brian, ninety-nine percent vegetarian, fancied the Margherita but he didn't want to appear unmanly so he told Jean he'd had a big steak for his dinner and couldn't face another morsel of meat.

'You look well. All dressed up.'

'I'd almost forgotten how to put lipstick on.'

'It looks good. It matches your hair. I've only ever seen you in your work clothes.'

'I said to myself as I charged over here through the park that I wasn't going to talk about work.'

'I said the same. Never mind work. Although I do have a snippet of information about Aisha's neighbour, but it can wait for another time.'

'You'd better tell me now. I'll only be thinking about them both.'

'I called round at the house on Racecommon Road where the flat is, pretending to look for work. I met the landlord. I got a bit of a shock. It was my old mate Spike. You met him in the beer garden at the Miners Arms. That afternoon when you'd just finished training. The one with the shaved head.'

'How could I forget. What did he say?'

'Not much. But I saw three women up at one of the bedroom windows. I think they were Asian and they didn't look too happy.'

'One of them might have been Aisha's friend.'

'That's what I thought. It's a bit of a dump. It looks like they've crammed a few tenants in. Something dodgy's going on. But Spike's a bit of a hard case and I didn't fancy pressing him. He's a great bloke but he's unpredictable. While I was there, two dodgy characters turned up on a scooter and then another one pulled up in a big fancy motor. I left quick smart.'

'I'll mention it to Jon.'

'Jon?'

'Jon Hunt, the owner of Woodland House and the other two care homes.'

'Oh I remember. Harry mentioned his name. He says he's a decent bloke.'

'He is. And so is his wife. They're obviously in it to make a profit, but they're very professional and caring. They're not all like that. There's a care home on the other side of Brodworth. It's been there for years. It was run by a local family and it had a very good reputation. But then a few years ago it was taken over by a private equity firm from somewhere down south we were told. The old manager and a lot of the existing staff left. It's not the same. We heard the other day the new manager and her staff are under investigation for mistreating the residents.'

'The rot starts at the top.'

'I just hope Jon and his wife never sell out to a private equity firm. They look after us and we look after the residents.'

'That's good to know.'

'Jon knows a lot of people in the care home business so he might know something about accommodation for care workers.'

'Let's hope so.'

'I'll not say anything to Aisha just yet. Let's see what Jon has to say.'

'Right, that's enough about work. Let's get to know each other. Do you want to go first? What's your life story?'

'It's not very exciting.'

'It will be to me.'

Jean took a drink of wine. Brian stared at the trace of red lips left behind on the glass. It was an image he used to see every Saturday night in town and think nothing of. Now he couldn't stop thinking about Susan.

'I left school at sixteen,' Jean said. 'I hated the place. I'm not in the least bit academic. The teachers were okay, well most of them, but it wasn't for me. I got set on at Shaw's, the sewing factory on Doncaster Road and I was there for six years. I loved it. Some great lasses worked there. We had a brilliant time.'

'That factory's been going some time. I had to do a job there once when I was an apprentice joiner back in the eighties. I spent a full day at the place. I was a fresh faced young lad, wet behind the ears. Those women gave me some right stick.'

'We showed no mercy whenever a man, especially a young man, came into the factory. It was all women and girls on the factory floor. There were only half a dozen men there, the bosses. They had their own little office. We hardly ever saw them. Boy did we make it count. Pit language? You've heard nothing.'

'I still get embarrassed when I think about that day I spent there. Walking up and down past all those women

115

and girls at their machines.' Brian shook his head and his cheeks tingled. 'But it did me good. Building site banter was a doddle after that. Sorry, Jean. I interrupted you. I'm always doing that.'

'That's okay. It didn't feel like you were interrupting.'

'I'm just interested in you. I've forgotten how to...'

'Chat up a bird?'

'No. Talk to a woman. Listen to a woman.'

'I met a man while I was at the sewing factory, he worked at Brown's glassworks, and before I knew it I was pregnant and married.'

'In that order?'

'Sadly. I don't talk about him. Let's just say it was a miserable two years. He didn't want me to keep on working, not even part time. I really missed the camaraderie of being with those lasses. We were like sisters. My lad, Nathan, for all the trouble he's brought on me, saved my sanity. Looking after him on my own when we split up took up all of my time and attention but it stopped me feeling sorry for myself.'

'We never had kids – me and Susan. It was just something we never really fancied. Both sides of our families have kids. Jeff's got two. We thought there were enough of them running around. We were very lucky as a couple. We got on well from the day we first met right up to the day she passed away, five years ago.'

'Five years. That's tough.'

'I've no idea what it must be like to have kids or to live in an unhappy marriage.'

The waiter brought the pizzas and asked if they needed any olive oil or black pepper. They smiled and said they were fine. As the waiter turned away, two women at a table nearby stared at them. The women raised their eyebrows and nodded a few times and their men turned to look. Jean smiled back.

'That's made their day. Friday night. Jean spotted in the Miners Arms with a man.'

Only one or two faces were familiar to Brian, people he might nod to if he passed them on the street. What would he say if Malc suddenly popped up from under a table?

'It builds your character if nothing else,' Jean said. 'A bad marriage. And a lad who keeps going off the rails. But I'm not complaining.'

'He sounds a handful, young Nathan.'

'He's nearly twenty now. I'm hoping he'll settle down a bit now he's met Chloe. She seems okay, level headed, assertive. She's training to be a hairdresser. And she's got a lovely little girl.' Jean smiled as she tore off a segment of pizza. 'Little Summer. She's only two.'

Brian took his time dividing up his pizza with the little cutting wheel the waiter had given him. It meant he could avoid eye contact with Jean while he asked her an important question.

'Is the man you don't talk about still around?'

'Somewhere. I've no idea and no interest. We got divorced just after Nathan's fifth birthday.'

'How did the young lad take it?'

'I could blame all his troubles at school, and with the police, on the man we don't talk about, but I didn't help matters. It took some getting over, the unhappy period, and I could have been a better mother.'

'From where I'm sitting, Nathan couldn't have had a better mother.'

Jean looked away but not before her eyes glistened under the lights. It was either tears or the chilli on her pizza.

'You care for people. You treat them with respect. That's one of the things that attracted me to you. As well as being damn good looking, of course.'

Jean laughed quietly to herself and said, 'I'll take that compliment. It's been a while since I had one.'

'How long have you been a care worker?'

'Almost four years, and I've loved every minute of it, even though we have to work our socks off. A bit more money from the local authority for the home and the residents, a bit more money and training for us all, and a few more staff would improve things greatly. It might stop the high turnover.'

'I've heard people say carers could earn more money stacking shelves in a supermarket.'

'It's true. I've got nothing against people who stack shelves – I did it myself for a few years at the co-op while Nathan was still at school. But when caring's in your blood you put up with a lot of the hardship that comes with being a care worker. That's why the football is so important to us. It keeps us healthy in mind and body. It's better than any medicine. It brings everybody together; the staff, the residents, the visitors, and the community. Carers United is the glue.'

'Let's drink to that,' Brian said, and they touched glasses.

'So, that's my life story. What about you?'

'My dad was a miner for a few years. Then when the pits shut he got a job as a carpet fitter and eventually ended up working for the highways. My mother gave up work to look after me and our Jeff, I did an apprenticeship to be a joiner, and I've been messing about with wood ever since.'

'Short and sweet.'

'Before I got married, all I did was go to work and play football. Me and my mates went to pubs and to any parties we could find. That's all I was interested in. I was young, carefree and daft.'

'Sounds like Nathan.'

'It was good fun, though. Then when I was twenty eight I got married, to Susan. We met in a pub in town. We bought a house and did it up over the years, and I gradually stopped going out with my mates. I seemed to spend most of my time doing DIY around the house. I know, it's grey and boring, but it saved me and Susan a load of money and it meant we could have some great holidays. We lived for our holidays.'

'And now?'

'Since Susan died I've filled my life with work, work and more work.'

'What did Susan do?'

'She worked at Brodworth General Hospital since leaving school, in the office. We were married for twenty years.'

Brian was doing too much chattering again. It must be first date nerves. Jean had mentioned Nathan a few times during their meal. You didn't need to be a psychologist to realise her son was at the front of her mind.

'I could have ended up in trouble with the police every week when I was growing up; driving when I'd had a few too many, pinching tools and materials off building sites, syphoning petrol when we couldn't afford to buy any. Me and my mates once nicked a car when we'd been to Sheffield for a night out and didn't fancy the long walk home. We did all the things lads with any ounce of spirit do when they're young, and we managed not to get caught. We were lucky. It's called growing up.'

'If I'd had a daughter I think I would have handled bringing her up on my own a lot better. I know what young girls get up to. We would have talked about things. But with Nathan...'

'He's missed out on a dad by the sounds of it. Maybe he's angry. It's understandable.'

Jean laughed.

'He's certainly angry all right. Apart from when he's with Chloe and Summer or when he's looking after his pigeons.'

'Pigeons.'

'He's decided he wants to race pigeons, now.'

'My granddad used to race pigeons.'

'I suppose I should be grateful he's found something he likes doing other than getting into trouble.'

'Some people never find something they like doing.'

'I feel angry with myself sometimes. I can organise my staff, I can coach a football team, but when it comes to handling Nathan...'

They shared a chocolate ice cream served in a tall glass and laughed at the intimacy of touching spoons and messy mouths. When the waiter started to clear the tables, Brian offered to walk Jean home.

The sun had dropped behind the houses but it was still light. In the park, the red, blue, and white begonias in the flower bed had taken on a different shade, drained but just as wonderful. A few couples were out, strolling along the path, hand in hand, passing other couples and nodding. Brian and Jean walked a yard apart but they stared into each other's eyes when they spoke, especially when they talked about football. Brian wanted to grab Jean's hand and run around the park. Find a football and kick it as high as the moon. Maybe Jean wanted to do the same.

They stopped outside Jean's house. The curtains in the front room were open and a soft light lit up the window. The attached semi next door was in darkness. As they were standing in front of the gate, a car shot out of the estate at the end of the road. The vehicle spun round, its tyres skidding and screeching, and disappeared into the back streets where it had come from.

'They're always doing that,' Jean said. 'They wait until everybody's gone to bed.'

'Handbrake turns. It's the latest craze. We had skateboards.'

'Do you want to come in for a coffee?'

'Love to.'

Jean put the kettle on and Brian sat on the sofa in the front room. There was a photograph on the TV cabinet of Jean and a young boy, presumably Nathan, by her side. It was the only photograph on display. On the dining table in a corner at the back of the room there was a bunch of flowers in a glass vase. Red roses. Brian cursed himself. He would bring some next time. If there was a next time.

Jean put her head round the kitchen door. 'Milk and sugar? Oh I remember, you like it black.'

Brian smiled. Woodland House seemed five hundred miles away not five hundred yards.

Jean put the drinks on the coffee table and sat next to Brian on the sofa. He didn't know where to put his hands so he picked up his drink and took a sip even though it nearly scalded his mouth.

'I take it that's Nathan?'

'He's seven there.'

'He looks like a little angel.'

'He always does on photographs.'

'I'd like to meet him sometime.'

'He's staying at Chloe's tonight.'

Brian put his coffee down and held Jean's hand.

'I've really enjoyed tonight, Jean. I was as nervous as hell walking into the Miners. I was like a kid on a first date. But it's been brilliant.'

'It has. I feel safe with you. I know I come across as tough and self-assured at work but it's all a show. I need somebody to hold my hand just as much as anybody else.'

They kissed, their arms wrapped around each other, the softness and warmth of Jean's body through her thin dress pressing against his chest. There was a clatter. Somebody laughed. Jean jumped up and straightened her dress.

'It's our bloody Nathan.'

Brian picked up his coffee and sat with his arm over the back of the sofa. Nathan came into the front room followed by Chloe, both wearing shorts and baseball caps. Summer was fast asleep in her mother's arms, the child's head resting against her mother's cheek.

'I thought you were staying at Chloe's tonight?'

'I can see you did. What's going on? Who's this?'

'This is Brian. Brian this is Nathan, and Chloe and little Summer.'

Brian stood up and held out his hand.

'Hi Nathan. Pleased to meet you.'

Nathan took his baseball cap off and threw it into the depression on the sofa where his mother had been sitting.

'If you're going to start messing around, Mam, you could at least pick somebody your own age.'

Brian sighed and lowered his outstretched hand.

'Brian's a friend of mine. We've been out for a meal in the Miners Arms and now we're just having a coffee.'

Chloe passed Summer over to Jean. The little girl stirred then fell silent as Jean held her close to her body.

'Anyway. Why am I defending myself? We've been out on a date. We're adults. It happens.'

'Good for you, Jean,' Chloe said, and she sat down on the leather armchair at the side of the gas fire. 'Can I put the telly on? See who got through on Up on the Stage. I'm hoping it's Lucinda and Simon.'

'Me too,' Brian said, and he winked at Jean and sat back down.

Nathan took two cans of beer out of the fridge and handed one to Chloe. She made room for Nathan on the leather chair then swung her long suntanned legs over his lap.

'I'll take Summer to bed,' Jean said. 'I'll be back in a minute.'

All eyes were on the TV screen but Brian and Nathan were assessing each other.

'Your mam tells me you're into racing pigeons, Nathan. Are they homers or milers?'

'Homers,' Nathan said still watching the TV. 'I use them to deliver drugs. It's the new county line method.'

'Nathan, stop it. Be nice to Brian.'

'Well it's cheaper than using cars and young kids.'

Nathan didn't know whether to shake his head at this stranger's naivety or totally ignore him.

'Hooray,' Chloe said. 'They've got through. I knew they would. Lucinda was twelve before she could walk.'

'My granddad used to race pigeons,' Brian said. 'Milers. I used to help him train them when I was a nipper. I loved it. He never fancied homers. He said they needed a lot more time and effort to get them trained up.'

Nathan took a swig of beer from his can. Chloe kissed him on the cheek.

'You love training them, don't you, Nathan.'

'Better than watching the telly all day long.'

'Where do you keep them?' Brian said.

'At my mate's,' Nathan said still looking at the TV.

'And they're building a big hut to keep them in,' Chloe said.

'It's a loft not a hut.'

'Same thing.'

'And it's not that big.'

'Are you and your mate doing it yourselves?' Brian said.

'Who else is going to do it?'

'If it's a big job I could give you a hand. I specialise in loft conversions.'

Nathan pulled a face. Jean came into the room. She must have been listening through the partially closed door.

'Brian's a joiner.'

'There you are, Nathan,' Chloe said. 'I told you you'd get lucky one day.'

'Just give me a shout. I've got all the tools and I've loads of spare wood at home. Probably enough to build ten pigeon lofts. It wouldn't cost you a penny.'

Chloe kissed Nathan on the cheek again and although he tried to turn away there was a hint of a crack in the hard shell.

Brian stood up and Jean took his empty cup off him.

'Right, Jean. I'd better be getting off.'

Chloe jumped off Nathan's lap and shook Brian's hand. When Brian held out his hand to Nathan, the young lad reluctantly took it.

Outside, Jean opened the garden gate. The clang of the little sneck echoed like a dropped spanner in the empty street.

'I really enjoyed meeting Nathan and Chloe tonight, even though I might have landed myself with a job to build a pigeon loft for the lad.'

'That was good of you.'

'I meant it. Let me know if he wants me to give him a hand.'

The moon was out and the clouds around it were thin and static. The outline of the bandstand and the clock half a mile away in the park stood out against the dark sky.

'It's five to twelve already.'

'It always is round here.'

A cat came out of next door's gate, stopped half way across the road, looked long enough to disregard the two of them then disappeared into the gate opposite.

'I'd better be off.'

'I've really enjoyed tonight, Brian.'

'Me too. It's been great. I'll probably catch you next week when I call round to see my dad.'

'I'll look forward to it.'

They kissed goodnight and Brian walked home.

15

It was a quarter past seven on Tuesday night and the bandstand clock showed five to twelve. The Carers United squad, or at least those who were fit and not working shifts, were training in Woodland Park, a few days after the team's victory in the rematch against Masons FC at their Sheffield ground. Brian, Malc and Harry the handyman had been to the rematch, and were now analysing the game as they watched the players train. Jean was taking the training session. She was full of energy, shouting instructions, blowing her whistle, keeping up with the young players, laughing when they laughed. She never looked over to where Brian was standing and he knew why.

He hadn't told Malc, or anybody else about his date with Jean. But his best mate would have noticed a change in his behaviour. Noticed how much happier he was, how light his footsteps were. He never missed a thing. Brian would tell him soon, of course. Malc was always telling him it was time he went out and found another woman. But Malc and his wife Pauline were very close to Susan. He would have to be careful. And, come on, it was only a date.

'What do you think, Brian?'

Jean's image merged with Susan's then disappeared. Malc and Harry were looking at him in silence. How long had they been waiting for his response?

'What was that? I missed it.'

Malc raised his eyebrows as though he was looking over a pair of reading glasses.

'I said I thought it was a close game, the rematch.'

'Yes. So did I.'

Malc knew. The nod and the knowing smile said it all. Said it was okay. What a relief. What a friend. Brian looked away. He was already on a foursome holiday with Jean, Malc and Pauline.

It had been a close game with the score at three all for most of the second half. That was until Sheila controlled a long clearance from Kalina and, using her low centre of gravity and speed over ten yards, ran through the Masons FC defence and with a delicate chip over their advancing goalkeeper scored a rare goal that won the game. Her backward somersault and star jump delighted the crowd.

The three match analysts agreed Carers United were the better team on the day. Harry, having seen the squad formed from scratch only six months earlier, thought they had improved no end.

'They'll give their all when they play the New Acorn. I hope it takes place here in the park, and I hope Jean can sort the shifts out and field her best side.'

'I'm looking forward to the game,' Brian said. 'Are you coming to the meeting in the Miners Arms after the training session with us?'

'I am. Jean's well prepared.'

'She'll need to be,' Malc said. 'Duggan might be there.'

Two women, out walking with a child by their side in a yellow harness, altered the course of their evening stroll and stopped at the side of the red, blue, and white begonias to watch the women training. Nearby in the bandstand, a teenage courting couple were doing what teenage courting couples do partially hidden behind a pillar. In the children's play area, three young lads were standing up on the swings, forcing the seats down and up through the air, pushing the swings and themselves to the limit. Brian held his breath every time the chains slackened and the youngsters hung motionless in mid-air. Did they ever, accidentally or through bravado, go over the top? When he and Jeff were the same age as those youngsters it was Jeff who was the daredevil, risking his neck on the swings, the tree tops and the deep end of the swimming pool. Brian would keep his feet on the ground and warn his younger brother to be careful.

'I've heard you mention him before,' Harry said. 'Is he in your team?'

'Duggan?' Brian said. 'No. He's all on to walk.'

'But he thinks he's in charge,' Malc said.

'He's a bit of a handful at times but he has his good sides.'

'I've not seen them.'

'For a start, he's definitely a winner. When we were playing football he never gave up, even when we were two nil down with a minute to go. He was a brilliant goalkeeper before he broke his back.'

'I'll give you that,' Malc said. 'But he's too aggressive for me. I don't get on with him.'

'We've all got a good and a bad side,' Harry said. 'There was only one man with no bad side and look what they did to him.'

A car pulled into the car park and Duggan and Pete got out and came down the path towards them.

'That's a blow,' Malc said. 'I was hoping he might have forgotten about the meeting.'

128

Back on the field, the squad were practising a new defensive formation down their left flank to cover a gap exploited by Masons FC. It had led to them conceding two goals. Central to the new approach was to get the defenders to stop giving the ball away when under pressure. Brian, Malc and Harry agreed with Jean's analysis. But the new tactic wasn't working. The long grass made it difficult to play accurate short passes out of defence, and Kalina, standing in goal between two cones, and Mahsa, Helen and Anne at the back were struggling to make progress. Most of their attempts were intercepted by attackers, Gloria, Aisha and Sheila whose sole purpose was to chase and harass and never give up running. Despite the repetition and the frustrated swearing from Anne and Helen none of the players wanted the drill to end until they had mastered the new approach.

Brian turned to Duggan and Pete, now standing next to them on the touch line.

'You've got to give it to the women, they're keen to learn.'

'And top marks for enthusiasm,' Malc said. 'They're fitter than I remember.'

Duggan must have been watching a different training session.

'Apart from that little one upfront they play like carthorses. I know she's black but she's not bad. She's got good ball control, I'll give her that.'

Pete agreed, of course and he spoke into Brian's ear in a voice loud enough for them all to hear.

'It must be with kicking all those mangoes around in the jungle.'

'That's not funny, Pete,' Brian said.

Duggan thought it was and he told Brian to lighten up. It was only a joke. A bit like watching these women train.

Harry's eyes were focussed on the training but he heard Duggan's comment.

'That's not a very nice thing to say, if I may say so.'

'What's it got to do with you, granddad?'

Duggan gave his warning smile and the stare that said somebody had better tell that old bloke to keep his mouth shut.

'Hey, come on Tommy,' Brian said. 'Harry's the handyman at the home, and the bag man for the team. He doesn't mean any harm.'

Duggan said nothing and although he looked away, he retained his hammer-cocked smile. Brian shook his head at Harry to tell him not to be drawn. He made a note to have a word with him later, and make it clear it was best not to tangle with Tommy Duggan.

After a few minutes, the two women with the child in the yellow harness turned away from the training session and continued their walk through the park. At the same time, the courting couple suspended their canoodling and left the relative privacy of the bandstand and walked towards Brian's group. The girl was giggling and pawing the lad and he was trying to look uninterested. As they came closer, the girl screamed and everyone turned to see what the hell had happened. She was up on her toes, trying her best to hide behind her boyfriend who was telling her to calm down. She gripped his arm and pointed to something scurrying through the grass. Harry was the first in the group to see the creature.

'It's only a bank vole, love. It'll not hurt you,' and he walked towards it with his hands open ready to usher it to the safety of the longer grass.

Brian and Malc smiled at the sight of the five foot six girl hiding from a three inch chestnut brown rodent. Then Duggan ran at the vole and kicked it as hard as he could, killing it. He came back to the group with a bully's smile on his face, like a big schoolboy who has just pulled a chair from under the smallest kid in school. Everybody went quiet, including the terrified girl. Duggan carried on watching the women train without saying a word.

At the end of the training session the squad came over to the touch line and collected their tops and leggings and wiped the sweat from their foreheads and arms.

Gloria said, 'We look like drownded rats.'

Mahsa untied the knot holding her long hair in place and the shiny black tresses fell around her shoulders.

'Free hair shampoos for everyone the next time I'm in Woodland House.'

***

Back at the car park the women's squad said goodnight. Half went home and half went into work. Brian, Malc, Duggan and Pete followed Jean and Harry into the Miners Arms across the road from the park entrance. Jean had already reserved a table near the window in the dining area, knowing the pub would be busy by the time they finished training. She was right. Almost every table was taken with families eating pasta, pizzas, chips, curry, or baked potatoes. It was cosy and warm in the dining area, too warm with the door closed. You could identify every individual meal on each table, even with your eyes closed, if you breathed in hard enough and analysed the various distinctive aromas. The couple on the next table were already onto the sweet course, apple pie and custard. The smell of cinnamon and nutmeg reminded Brian of the puddings his mother used to make.

Duggan and Pete ordered a pint and everyone else ordered coffee. Brian, being the common link between Carers United and the New Acorn, formally introduced Duggan and Pete to Jean and Harry. Jean moved the reserved sign on the table out of the way, put her notebook and pen down in front of her and opened the meeting. Brian winked at Malc and they both settled into their chairs.

'Right,' Jean said. 'I think we all know why we're here but just to repeat, the purpose of this meeting is to organise the details of the big match, as everyone seems to be calling it now, between Carers United and the New Acorn.'

'Word's getting round,' Brian said.

Duggan folded his arms and looked anywhere except at Jean, his mouth tight shut. Pete adopted the same body language. He wouldn't say a thing until Duggan had set out his own position.

'We need to sort out a date first because most of my girls work shifts and I can only get a team together on certain days. Tuesday nights are best for us.'

'Can't do Tuesdays,' Duggan said. 'We've got into the habit of training on Wednesdays. That's the only night we can do midweek. What's wrong with the weekend?'

'We can make Saturday afternoon at a push. But it would be difficult with the shift patterns. I could do it if we had to.'

'We've only had a couple of training sessions, Tommy,' Brian said. 'Nothing's been fixed. I'm sure the lads are flexible enough to make a Tuesday night just for one single game.'

Duggan took a drink of lager and banged his glass down on the table.

'Let's go for Saturday,' he said. 'Where are we going to play?'

'Hang on,' Jean said. 'We'll come to the location in a bit. Which Saturday are we looking at?'

Malc pulled up the diary on his phone.

'How about the last Saturday of the month? That'll give us time to do a bit more training. Our boys certainly could do with a couple more training sessions to get everybody into some sort of shape.'

'We're still recovering from the last training session we had,' Brian said. 'I've been walking around like a robot for five days. How does the last Saturday of the month sound to you, Jean?'

Jean carried her diary in her head. Back at the care home, if anybody asked about the staff rota, she would look up at the ceiling for a few seconds then give a quick, accurate answer. Brian never once saw her consult a rota sheet or open up her diary. Impressive.

After a few seconds staring at the ceiling Jean made her decision.

'The last Saturday of the month will be fine for us.'

'I'll go with that as long as all my team can make it. I'll let you know.'

Brian sat back and stroked his chin. How come all of a sudden, Duggan was the coach of the New Acorn team? Malc was thinking the same thing.

'Six o'clock kick-off?' Jean said. 'Twenty minutes each way?' Everyone nodded and Jean put the date and time in her notebook. 'Right. Location. Where shall we play the match?'

This time Duggan came straight in.

'It's got to be on Aspinal Rec's training ground. It's a no-brainer. It's the ideal size for a seven-a-side football match. It's got proper goalposts and nets, and there's a ten foot fence all around it so we'll not spend half the game fetching the ball back. And it's artificial turf so even if it pisses it down all week we'll still be able to play on it.'

'Sounds like a good pitch. Has it got any changing rooms?'

'It's got plenty of benches. Bring a screen.'

Pete laughed at Duggan's quick wit.

'Are there any toilets?'

'No. We'll bring plenty of buckets to piss in.' Duggan laughed so loud at his own humour the couple on the next table stopped eating their apple pie and custard and turned round to see what was so funny. Then Duggan's laughing face turned into a grimace. He took a deep breath, stretched out his leg, and stuck his knuckles into his back.

'Are you okay, Tommy?' Pete said.

Duggan wiped his brow and said nothing.

Jean gave him a few seconds to recover.

'You say it's enclosed. If we get a lot of spectators turning up on the evening, which we might do, is there somewhere for them all to stand and watch without their view being obstructed by fencing?'

Jean seemed well prepared, even by her standards, and then the penny dropped. Of course. The stranger they'd seen making notes in the car park at Aspinal Rec when they were training wasn't a coach from an over-fifties club after all. Good old Harry.

Duggan's face went from ashen to crimson and he unfolded his arms and gripped the edge of the table.

'What do you want, Wembley? Aspinal Rec is the best set up in Brodworth by a mile.'

'I'm just checking. The other thing is if we play at Aspinal Rec, where you've been training your team will have an unfair advantage over our team. It's not a neutral ground.'

'Not a neutral ground. What do think we're playing, a UEFA Champions League final! It's a poxy little game against a poxy little team of women.'

Two men drinking at the bar looked across when they heard the raised voice and Brian sensed trouble. Jean's reasoning was sound, but he didn't want to upset Duggan. The man would only go around the New Acorn squad one by one telling them Jean was a nutcase, and the idea of playing Carers United was pathetic, just as he'd said right from the beginning. Duggen wouldn't rest. He would do everything he could to make sure the contest never took place. If it was anybody but Duggan, Brian would tell them to calm down. Was he frightened of the man? Frightened he might be confronted and threatened right here in front of Jean? Shown up. Asked to step outside. Duggan had form.

'Let's not get too excited,' Brian said. 'I think Jean makes some fair points. But Tommy's right. Aspinal Rec's training pitch itself is perfect for a seven-a-side game of football. Does anybody know where we might find another ground with a decent surface, but with none of the problems Jean has just highlighted?'

'If you say it doesn't matter if it's a neutral ground or not,' Jean said, 'why don't we play the match in Woodland Park?'

Duggan put his head in his hands then looked through his open fingers.

'Tell me you're joking. That's not a football field. It's a rubbish tip. You haven't even got any goal posts. You've no toilets there, neither. And you're on about changing rooms. Where's everybody going to get changed in a park? In the bandstand? Both teams stripping off with a towel wrapped round their arses.'

'It'd be like being on the beach, Tommy,' Pete said. 'That would bring in the crowds. They'd all be waiting for somebody's towel to fall off.'

Pete laughed. Nobody else did and Jean's face never altered. She remained business-like. No smiling. No leaning back when Duggan leaned forward. She had it all. Getting her staff to work well together. Handling upset relatives with tact, diplomacy and empathy. Treating residents with respect. Liaising with the doctors, the hospital, the charities. And now getting the best deal for the women's football team. Brian's heart swelled, he could feel it pressing against his throat.

'Don't worry about nets or changing rooms or toilets,' Jean said. 'We'll sort them out. And we'll sort out the grass as well. It'll all be up to scratch by the time we play the match. I can guarantee it. And as you've just said, it's not as though it's a UEFA Champions League final. It's just a little game of seven-a-side football, women against men. We'd be more than happy to play you in Woodland Park.'

Brian and Malc nodded and Harry gave a thumbs up.

Duggan folded his arms again and sat back in his chair.

'Fine, but I think you're making a big mistake. It's amateurish.'

'Pete? What about you?'

Pete looked at Duggan for a steer but he got no response. Jean gave him plenty of time to answer.

'If Tommy's happy with that, then I suppose that's okay.'

'Woodland Park it is, then.'

It didn't take long for the colour of Duggan's cheeks to return to normal. He had lost the argument over the ground for now but he was back in control of himself, calculating and plotting. He wouldn't let the defeat over the venue go by without trying to get his revenge. Brian made another mental note, this time to warn Jean about Duggan's likely reaction.

'What are we doing about a referee?'

'That's a good point, Tommy.' Brian said. 'I hadn't thought about a referee. Had you, Jean?'

'I've been thinking about it.'

'I know an ex professional referee,' Duggan said. 'He used to referee in League One. He'd be fair and neutral. I'll ask him if he'll referee the game.'

An ex-professional referee? Fair and neutral? Duggan must be getting worried about the match. His ego wouldn't be able to cope with losing to a team of women, not with his reputation as a winner and the best goalkeeper in Brodworth. What was he scheming now?

'That sounds good,' Jean said. 'We can agree the rules of the game with him on the day; off-sides, penalties and so on. What about the referee's assistants? We can provide one. Would you be able to provide the other?'

Duggan glanced at Pete, making him shift in his chair.

'We'll provide a linesman.'

'That's great,' Jean said. She closed her notebook and pushed her pen down the rings on the spine. 'Thanks for that. We've made good progress. The last thing for me and Harry, is to ask you if you're happy for us to use the game to raise money for Woodland House care home and for Clayton village? We do lots of charity events to raise money for the home and the village during the year. This would be a great chance to do some more fund raising.'

'It's up to you,' Duggan said, and he downed the last of his lager and wiped his lips. 'It's not my problem.'

Harry had been quiet throughout the meeting. He must have known Jean could handle Duggan and his bullying style without his help. Now he spoke with confidence.

'I've just had an idea. What about getting a trophy? It would make the game a bit special. If we could find somebody to present it to the winning team, somebody important, then it might attract a few more folk to the game. That would help us raise a bit more money for Woodland House and Clayton village.'

'Sounds good,' Jean said. 'Leave it with me. I'll see what I can do.'

'I've got another suggestion,' Brian said. 'Why don't both teams come back to my house for a drink straight after the game? It's only just down the road from the park. We could have a barbecue if the weather stays good.'

'Nice one, Brian,' Harry said. 'I like the idea of making it into more of a social event. You'd get a chance to see the other side of people.'

Duggan shrugged. Jean made a note of Brian's excellent suggestion and then closed the meeting.

***

The next morning, while Nathan was still in bed, Jean picked up her mobile and rang the first contact in her notebook.

'Is that Janice...? Hello, my dear. It's Jean from Carers United. You know those seven-a-side goal posts and nets you brought over to Woodland Park when you played us? Any chance I could borrow them one Saturday evening...?'

We're playing against a team of middle aged men who still think they can play football...That's great. It'll be good to see you again. How do you fancy being a referee's assistant...?'

Jean worked methodically down the list of contacts, ringing up each person and greeting them with bundles of bright, early morning energy.

Stan at Brodworth Chronicle, tick.

Duncan at the town council offices, tick.

Harriot at Supa Signs on the industrial estate a mile up the road from Woodland House, tick.

Lauren, secretary at Clayton Colliery brass band, tick.

Diane and Victoria, who each owned a cake shop on the high street, tick.

Tom, manager of the Co-op supermarket, tick.

And last on the list, Jon Hunt, owner of the three care homes, tick.

At ten o'clock Jean entered Woodland House, job done, shift begun.

16

Brian was standing on the third rung of the care home's unsteady aluminium stepladder with a box of coloured notice board pins in one hand, and a hammer in the other. He was helping Harry put the last of the bunting up in the corner of the big lounge downstairs. After the final pin went in, Brian climbed off the stepladder and stood back to inspect their work. They had managed, after a bit of clowning and creative spelling, to put the black letters on the coloured bunting in the correct order and now HAPPY BIRTHDAY hung down evenly with no twists or creases.

'How does that look, Harry?'

'Spot on, Brian. If ever you want a full time job here volunteering...'

'That could come sooner than I thought. I'm getting to that age when climbing onto a roof is like climbing up Mount Everest.'

The four birthday cards Brian's dad had been given were already up on the wall, clipped to a length of red ribbon and hanging down like a colourful necklace. Brian's card was on the right, a goalkeeper tipping a shot over the bar in front of a huge crowd. Next to that was a big sparkly card signed by all the staff at the care home. There was a card from Harry with a garden and a greenhouse on the front. The fourth card was from the fellow residents on his dad's floor. Brian had bought the card, and asked Mary and Arthur and all the others still capable of holding a pen if they would like to wish his dad a happy birthday. Brian showed Jean the signed card and both agreed the scratchy words were more poignant than any perfectly formed birthday greeting. When Mary and Arthur presented the card his dad clasped it to his chest and said, 'Thank you my friends.'

'Right, Harry. If you don't need me anymore, I'm off up to my dad's room to put some trimmings up while he's having his hair washed and his daily shave. Are you coming to his party this aft?'

'I'll be there. I've just got to fix a door lock in the lounge upstairs and cut the back lawn but I'll be there for one o'clock.'

'By the way, is Jean working today?'

'I don't think she is. It's her day off. But you know what she's like.'

When Brian stepped out of the lift, Aisha was vacuuming the carpet in the corridor outside his dad's room. She turned off the machine and pulled the cord clear of the open door.

'Hello, Brian. I understand it is your dad's birthday today.'

'It is, Aisha. We're having a party in the lounge downstairs this afternoon. If you pop in around one o'clock there'll be plenty of cakes and buns.'

'Thank you. I will try to get there for five minutes. Will there be cream buns?'

'Of course. I'll save one especially for you.'

Brian went into his dad's bedroom and left the door open while Aisha carried on vacuuming, the noise decreasing and the slack cord straightening as she worked her way down the corridor. Jean had given him permission to tape the coloured bunting to the pelmet above the window and then run it across to the wall behind the bed and back again. He was standing on the visitor's chair, his hair brushing the ceiling, deciding what to do with the spare ends of the bunting over the window, when Jean came in to the room. She was carrying a clear plastic bag full of incontinence pads. The bag was heavy and as big as a pillow but she managed to open the bathroom door, and without looking at Brian, said, 'Good Morning.'

'Good morning. Is there nothing you don't do in this place?'

'Jean of all trades, that's me. So is everyone else here. You have to be otherwise the place would come to a standstill.'

Jean disappeared into the bathroom and there was the double click of a cupboard door opening and closing. She came back into the bedroom and the bag was just as heavy. Her back was straight, and her fingers gripped with little effort, but there were dark circles under her eyes. Brian carried on fiddling with the bunting.

'I was hoping you might be in. Harry thought it might be your day off.'

'It is. I've just popped in to see if Kalina needs any help organising your dad's birthday party. It's the first time she's organised a party here at Woodlands.'

'You look tired.'

Jean put the bag down and cracked her fingers.

'Too much work.'

'I was going to ring the home to try and catch you in but I thought it best not to.'

'You could have done. I should have given you my mobile number.'

'I should have given you mine. I never thought. I'm a bit out of practice at this dating thing.'

142

'You seemed alright on the night. I had a great time.'

Brian nearly lost his balance.

'Me too. We ought to do it again.'

The two loose ends of bunting were different lengths but when he twisted them together and tied them into a knot you would never have known. He stepped off the chair and pushed it back under the bedside table, careful not to knock over his dad's photographs.

'What do think then? Not bad for a bloke.'

'What are you doing at Christmas? You'd come in handy at my house.'

'I don't put trimmings up at home. It brings back too many memories of the happy times I had there at Christmas with Susan.'

'What better reason for putting them up. Memories are precious.'

It was a bit uncomfortable, talking to Jean in a bedroom with only the two of them there, even with the door wide open. It wasn't like being in a hospital ward with machines and nurses and white coats everywhere. It was his dad's bedroom. The photos and the curtains from his dad's old house made it feel intimate, almost as though Jean was the visitor not him.

'I know. I should. But it would upset me too much.'

Jean was looking at the blue quilt on the bed, creased where he had been standing. It was a simple quilt. No frills or patterns. He bought it from a shop in Brodworth along with the matching pillow case. The attractive young woman who served him said it was unusual and lovely to see a man buying a quilt and a pillow case for an elderly parent. She'd smiled and cocked her head as though she felt sorry for him, a lonely middle-aged widower.

Jean pulled the edge of the quilt tight to smooth out the creases. Brian tried to give her a hand.

'I took my shoes off.'

'It's a good job.'

She smoothed the bottom end of the quilt with the flat of her hand, and Brian copied her action and smoothed the top end. They were close to each other, a bit too close for Brian, and they avoided each other's eyes and spoke to the bed. When their hands reached the middle section at the same time, Brian gave way.

The light caught the side of Jean's face as she plumped up the pillow, accentuating the downy fair hair on her cheek. It had been an intimate setting in the Miners Arms, but the lighting was much harsher than the midday sun now entering his dad's bedroom.

They swapped mobile phone numbers and smiled at each other, the little interchange as intimate as a kiss. How many years had passed since he exchanged contact details with a woman, other than to arrange a quote for a roofing job?

Aisha walked past the open door pushing her vacuum and said hello to both of them. Jean waited until she heard Aisha talking to someone further along the corridor.

'I told Jon Hunt about Aisha's friend and what you'd seen at the flat.'

'Good. What did he say?'

'He's come across that kind of thing before. He had a word with his contacts at the local authority, they're responsible for overseeing employment of care workers, and they told him it could be a scam run by dodgy agents and dodgy employers. Even involving dodgy care homes. The sponsorship should only cost a few hundred pounds, but some of these unscrupulous employers charge up to twenty five thousand pounds.'

'Chuffing hell. Aisha said her friend had been overcharged.'

'Most of the care workers caught up in this kind of scam can't afford to pay such a high sponsorship in one go, so they have to borrow money. Guess who offers to lend them the money and find them accommodation?'

'The dodgy agent?'

'Or the unscrupulous employer. The debt, including interest, has to be paid off out of the care worker's wage.'

'Bastards.'

'And they take their passports off them so they can't run away.'

'They've got them by the short and curlies.'

'The local authority's going to look into it. In some cases they've managed to arrange with care providers to take over the migrant workers sponsorship.'

'You mean take over their debt?'

'Apparently.'

'Wow.'

'Jon said he'd consider employing Aisha's friend if it turned out she was being mistreated.'

'What a hero.'

'But he has to be careful. He doesn't want to cross a dodgy agent or an unscrupulous employer, even if the police are involved.'

'I wouldn't want to either if that big Asian guy I saw when I called round is anything to go by.'

'The local authority told Jon that some landlords get in on the act as well.'

'I hope Spike's not in on any racket.'

'I'll let you know what Jon comes up with.'

'Caring people and uncaring people side by side. You can't believe it.'

'Anyway,' Jean said, shaking the plastic bag to settle the incontinence pads. 'Is your brother calling in to see your dad today on his birthday?'

'Unlikely. We're back to thinking about it. It's all getting a bit predictable.'

'I thought he might have visited on this special today.'

'So did I. But I've not heard a thing from him. He hasn't even given me a card to deliver.'

'Don't tell me if you don't want to, but why doesn't he want to visit your dad?'

'He does; that's the trouble. He was ten yards away from seeing him the other day. At the singing charity event. It's his wife, June who's stopping him. Something happened in the past between them both and my dad, don't ask me what it was, and now he's frightened to death to even talk about my dad in front of her. When I told him about the party you were planning, he said he knew my dad's birthday was coming up. He'd been thinking about it as he always does. But he said June gets depressed when the date's coming up, and she'd be watching what he got up to even more than usual.'

'That's sad.'

'I could fall out with our Jeff sometimes. He knows my dad's not going to have many more birthdays so you'd think he'd make the effort, just once.'

Jean gently put her hand on Brian's arm.

'Don't be too harsh on him, Brian. He is your brother.'

'I know he is. But as I keep saying, I'm not his keeper. He's old enough to look after himself.'

'What if he can't? Like your dad can't. All you can do is try to understand and not judge, even if you make a mess of it. And I've done a lot of that in the past. We're all responsible for the welfare of other people.'

Brian faltered. There it was again; Jean accusing him of being a couldn't-care-lesser. Okay, he admitted he cared for himself first. Look after number one as their dad used to say. If you can't look after yourself, who can you look after? Was that a selfish attitude? It didn't mean look after yourself and only yourself. Or did it?

'I think he's hoping the big match doesn't go ahead then he won't have to tell June he's playing against a team of care workers from my dad's home.'

'It sounds like he's struggling with himself, poor man.'

The bitterness had drained from Brian's tone but not from his words.

'He sides with Duggan every time there's a vote on anything to do with the game. I wouldn't put it past him if he said he was injured and couldn't play.'

'That's family for you.'

'Sure is.'

Brian wanted to change the subject, switch off the agitation building up inside. He was about to ask Jean how her team's preparations for the big match were going when his mobile phone rang. He pulled the Nokia out of his pocket and he had to look at the tiny screen twice.

'It's our Jeff,' he said, and he turned away from Jean. 'Hey up, bro...Of course I will. I'll come down straightaway.'

Jean was smiling when he put the phone away. Brian could only shake his head.

'He's got the bus here. He wants to come up.'

Jeff was standing in front of the entrance porch like a schoolboy outside the headmaster's office waiting to be caned. His face was grey, and he looked down as Brian clicked the security latch and held the door open for

147

him. Brian didn't speak. One clumsy word and Jeff would be back on the bus home. He signed his brother in and entered the security code. The mechanism clicked, he pushed the door open and they went into the home side by side.

Brian paused outside the hairdresser's room and put his arm across Jeff's chest. Their dad was sitting in a chair sideways on to the door with a white blanket around his shoulders. His cheeks and chin were covered with shaving foam and Mahsa was carefully scraping a razor around his Adam's apple. She was talking to him, telling him what she was doing, saying how popular he would be with everyone at his birthday party once she'd finished pampering him. Brian coughed and Mahsa straightened up and wiped the razor clean with a paper towel.

'Joe. Your Brian is here to see you.'

'And somebody else is here to see you, Dad. Somebody you haven't seen for a very long time.'

Brian stepped to one side, switching his gaze between his dad and his brother. Who would make the first move? Please, someone make the first move. Jeff took one step into the room and stood a handshake distance away from his dad, a thirty year distance.

'Hello, Dad.'

Their dad smiled but his eyes couldn't focus.

'It's our Jeff, Dad. He's come to see you on your birthday.'

'Jeff.'

'Our Jeff. Your son.'

Their dad's eyes slowly closed. He twitched and the white blanket shook. His eyes opened only to slowly close again and remain closed. Mahsa, sensing the tension, said she had just about finished smartening their dad up and suggested Brian and Jeff go upstairs. She would ask one of

148

the care workers to get a wheelchair and bring their dad up in the lift in ten minutes.

Brian took Jeff into their dad's bedroom rather than straight to the lounge. It would be a gentler introduction to the home's surroundings. He remembered the first time he visited the home, and walked into the little lounge and stepped into the intimidating semi-circle of staring, moaning, crying and half-awake residents. The first time he pulled up a stool and sat down next to his dad. The first time he tried to say the right things and ask the right questions without confusing or aggravating the old lad. Nobody told you how hard it would be, and what you could do to prepare yourself for the shock of seeing your loved one placed in a care home.

By the time they reached their dad's room Jeff was crying. Brian wanted to put his arms around his brother. The last time they hugged was five years ago at Susan's funeral. Before that they would have been at junior school. All those years. Gone.

Jeff picked up the photographs on the bedside table one at a time, each time moving his gaze to the one he was about to pick up before letting go of the one in his hand. He dwelt longest on the Skegness holiday snap and a smile returned for a few seconds and then the mood changed.

'I know I could have tried harder with my dad. I could have tackled him sooner before things got so deep seated. But what he did to me and June...That wasn't right. I don't think I'll ever be able to forgive him for that. I'm sure that's what killed my mother.'

How had he managed to keep whatever had caused the split inside for so long? And the extra cruelty of having to avoid their dad at their mother's funeral. What must that have been like?

Brian wanted to push the windows wide open, get some light and air into the room, some breathing space. The room with its en-suite toilet was a good size for a single person, bigger than the back bedroom at his dad's own house. It was one of the reasons Brian picked the home. The main reason being the good feeling he had about the staff when he first viewed the home.

The bed, the table and the built in wardrobe took up little space but now, with two adults standing a foot apart in front of the window, darkening the room, even the decorations he had put up seemed to be falling in on them.

'He looks so old,' Jeff said. 'He's no idea who I am anymore. I've missed so many years, and my kids have missed having a grandfather.'

Brian pulled a tissue out of the box at the side of the photographs and handed it to Jeff. They were little kids again, Brian bullying his little brother, making him cry the way big brothers do. Would life have been different if Jeff had been the eldest? He didn't believe in all that pseudo first child, middle child, last child stuff you read in magazines. But there was something in the way Jeff rarely looked happy, always suspicious, a deep sadness beneath the surface. They never mentioned the words 'mother's love' or 'father's love' at home, but Brian was the favourite child. Better than Jeff at football. Better than Jeff at school. Couldn't put a foot wrong.

They heard the lift door open followed by the cheery voice of Gloria saying, 'There we are, Joe.' She effortlessly pivoted the wheelchair on its back wheels and steered his dad, feet first, warm and cosy in his brown slippers through the doorway into the lounge.

'He's back up, Jeff. Shall we go and sit with him in the lounge for a few minutes?'

Their dad, smooth skinned, hair squeaky clean, was back in his chair between Arthur, looking pale again, and a bright Mary.

'Right,' Gloria said. 'There you are, Joe. Safe and sound and all spruced up.'

Brian's dad nodded and said thank you. His words were clear and deliberate. Brian's chest lifted.

'I love your dad's smile,' Gloria said. 'It brightens up the room.'

He was sure his dad still recognised him and possibly recognised Jeff as well. There was something in his eyes and smile. Jeff didn't seem so sure. He couldn't find a comfortable position on the little stool and he struggled to find something to say, even with Brian's prompting.

'Me and our Jeff's playing football against a team of women from here, Dad. Jean's the coach. They're a good side. We've seen them. Our Jeff's in goal, aren't you, Jeff.'

'Yes.'

Their dad looked directly into Brian and Jeff's eyes, searching for a connection. He knew something happy was being said and he smiled.

'Are you coming to watch us, Dad? You can play in goal in the second half if you want. The Tiger returns. Our Jeff'll lend you his boots.'

'I'll bring my own.'

Brian clapped his hands and laughed, but Jeff looked away and folded and unfolded his arms. After fifteen long, mostly silent minutes their dad closed his eyes and his head dropped slowly towards his chest.

Brian took his brother down to the ground floor and as they got out of the lift, Jeff said he was going to catch the bus home. He didn't feel strong enough to come to the party. He took a birthday card out of his inside pocket and asked Brian to wish their dad a happy birthday. Brian didn't judge his brother this time. It had been a short visit. An awkward visit. But it was a visit. The first contact between Jeff and his dad for thirty years and that was something to celebrate.

Brian walked through the quiet lounge to the corner set aside for the birthday party, smiling and nodding at any resident who stared at him. It was ten to one and he was the first there. Kalina had described how she proposed to set out the space so he had an idea of what the designated corner would look like. What he saw took him straight back to the parties he remembered as a child.

Red, yellow, and blue balloons had been tied to the back of the chairs and the window frame. Taped to the walls were sheets of A4 paper with paintings of flowers and birds and butterflies of every colour, all originals painted by the residents. Above a small drinks table set out with cans of beer, fruit juices and plastic tumblers, was a poster donated by the village bric-a-brac shop, of a cartoon life-sized French bar tender complete with beret and string bag of onions. A long folding table had been placed in the centre of the space. The white table cloth with its blue and pink napkins gave the simple structure an air of street party splendour. There were plates of cream buns and chocolate buns, and sandwiches sealed in plastic wrap. In the centre of the table was a birthday cake with ten candles pushed through the icing, baked on site by the cook.

When Brian asked Jean about the cost of the birthday party, she told him not to worry. All the bunting and banners would be reused for other birthday celebrations in the care home. Kalina would print 'Happy Birthday Joe' in black on a few white A4 sheets and stick them around the walls to personalise the celebrations so there was little cost there. Most of the confectionery had been donated the previous evening by the local Co-op. The sandwiches would cost next to nothing, because his dad and the other residents had prepared them that morning in an entertaining conveyor belt of butter spreading and layering of cheese and ham slices. Jean suggested Brian could contribute to the drinks at the bar, the cook's overtime and the few other incidental expenses out of his dad's pocket money. Brian signed the proper authorisation and made sure the home lost no money in putting on the celebration.

Now at five to one, Kalina arrived and turned on the tape deck and happy birthday music fell like tinsel from the little speakers high up on the wall and made the corner of the big lounge feel intimate and special.

By one o'clock all the guests had arrived. Brian was hoping Jean would be there but she had gone home, knackered, according to Kalina. His dad was sitting at the head of the table, centre stage. On either side, Arthur and Mary were laughing at each other as they tried to eat their buns without smearing cream all over their faces. Aisha was there too, taking a two minute break from cleaning and caring, wide-eyed, talking to Kalina, both enjoying a cream bun. Harry, squirting sanitiser onto his hands and apologising to everyone for the state of his fingernails, had popped in for a cup of tea and cake in between cutting the grass and watering the troughs and plant pots.

Brian worked his way around the scene, talking and eating, trying not to get chocolate and cream on Jeff's

153

card. When he reached the head of the table he shook his dad's hand.

'Happy birthday, Dad. And this is a happy birthday card from our Jeff.'

His dad struggled to get the card out of the envelope, even though Brian had left the flap wide open. After a few false starts, he pulled the card out and looked at the front and back and then tried to read the writing.

'Whose birthday is it?'

'It's yours, Dad. Look, our Jeff's written "All the best Dad from Jeff". Do you know how old you are, today?'

'Fifty three.'

The quick, certain answer made both of them laugh.

'You're seventy five, Dad. But you know what they say, you're only as old as you feel.'

'That's okay then.'

Brian hung Jeff's card over the smiling red ribbon on the wall, adding another gem to the necklace. Kalina lit the ten candles on the cake and everyone clapped as his dad made a valiant effort to blow them all out in one go. Everyone wished him a happy birthday and, as the wisps of black smoke drifted up from the extinguished candles, told him to make a wish. He looked confused but happy and Brian made a silent wish for him. 'Don't suffer, Dad. Stay as happy and content as you are right this minute. Lap up the love and care and attention you're getting from everybody around you. And if in time you forget who I am, don't worry – I'll never forget you.'

Aisha went back to her cleaning and caring duties, Harry went back to his gardening, and the partying went on till half past two (in the afternoon).

17

On the morning of the big match, Brian walked with Harry down the hill from the home towards Clayton village high street. Brian was carrying two cooler bags; one full of cheese and tomato sandwiches sealed in plastic wrap, the other heavy with bottles of water. Harry was pushing a wheelbarrow full of assorted equipment; a yard brush, a spade, four brand new flexible corner flags, a collection of tools, and a bucket. At the bottom of the hill, opposite the former Methodist Chapel, now the village boxing club, Harry put his barrow down.

'Jean's had a word with Rocky, the bloke who runs that boxing club and he said the men's team can get changed in the gym if they want.'

'Brilliant. She's a star. I'll let everybody know. Where are the women getting changed?'

'In the laundry room at Woodland House. When they've got changed we'll all walk down to the park together as one. Jean's taking this game seriously. She wants the girls to look professional when they walk through the village, no showing off but by the same token, no apologising. She wants them to be on the field fifteen minutes before kick-off to warm up, and to show respect to all those who have turned up to watch the game.'

Harry picked up his barrow and they set off again.

'I'll try and get our lot to do the same,' Brian said. 'The more I hear about Jean's approach to this game and to the women she works with, the more impressed I am. I rate her. I could work with somebody like Jean. I could have played football for her if she'd been my coach.'

'She rates you, as well.'

Brian straightened up. He could have carried three cooler bags.

The Saturday morning rush to the shops was nearly over but they decided not to risk dashing across the road with the wheelbarrow and its unsteady load and instead walked towards the zebra crossing opposite the Co-op. Harry paused outside the town's food bank.

'Have you seen this?' He pointed to the poster in the window. 'There's one in every shop on the high street.'

'Wow. We're famous. What an advert for football. That's clever, advertising the match as the climax to a family day out.'

'That was Jon Hunt's idea. He's just bought the lasses a new football strip for the match – purple shirts, black shorts and purple socks with white double stripes.'

'Nice.'

'The girls picked it.'

'I can't believe it's finally happening tonight. All this from Jean's challenge to play a game of football against a team of has-beens.'

Harry lifted up his baseball cap and wiped his forehead with the back of his hand.

'I hope it cools down a bit by six o'clock for the lasses.'

'I hope it does. I never liked playing in the heat.'

Brian offered to swap the two cooler bags for the wheelbarrow, but Harry stiffened his back and arms, tucked his chin in, and picked up the heavy load.

'No, you're right. I like the exercise. It keeps me young.'

A car stopped at the zebra crossing. Harry set off across the road like a greyhound out of the traps, and Brian had to lift his two bags higher and wider and stride out to keep up with him. They were side by side again when they reached the gravel path into the park.

'It's about time they got that clock fixed,' Brian said. 'It throws me out every time I see it.'

'That old clock's been stuck on five to twelve for as long as I can remember. It's comforting in a way. Not many things make time standstill. If the council ever get round to fixing it, I think everybody in Clayton would put a complaint in.'

'Well at least it's right twice a day.'

The air, full of eye-itching pollen from new mown grass, was sticky and hot. They reached the flower bed and the view of the park opened up. The green tractor pulling the rotating cutter was heading away from them towards the bandstand. The spinning rollers, at least two metres wider than the tractor, sent grass clippings and daisy heads into the air like cars throwing up spray in the rain. The wide combination turned round in a big sweep and headed back towards them.

Harry put his wheelbarrow down next to the children's play area and wiped his hands down his overalls. Brian stored his two cooler bags under one of the wooden park benches out of the sun.

'He's doing a good job of cutting that grass, Harry. How long would it have taken you to do that with your push-me-pull-me?'

'More years than I've got left on this earth. Good old Jean.'

The tractor stopped mid pitch opposite the play area. The cab door opened and the driver climbed out and waved Harry over.

'Come on. It's my old mate Bill from the council. He'll have brought the line marking machine for us. Bring a couple of those sandwiches and a bottle of water, Brian. He'll be ready for his morning break.'

There was a white tide mark of salt and sweat on the front edge of Bill's brown baseball cap. Harry and Brian greeted him and he lifted the peak and cooled his white bald head. Bill was wearing orange council overalls and dark brown rigger boots, and having just got out of the heat and the confines of the tractor cab he looked, as Brian's mother used to say, like a wet lettuce. Harry and Brian helped Bill lift the line marking roller, half the size of a wheelbarrow and twice the weight, plus the bag of calcium carbonate, out of the tractor and Bill showed Harry how much water to add to the powder.

'And keep your fingers out of the rollers until I come over. I don't suppose you've brought any gloves and goggles with you.'

'I've brought my gardening gloves,' Harry said. 'I didn't think about goggles. Won't my glasses do?'

'Council orders, Harry. Health and safety. Don't worry. I've brought a spare pair.'

Brian handed Bill the bottle of chilled water and the two sandwiches, cold and firm in their plastic wrap.

'Here you are, mate. You look as though you could do with a rest.'

'That's grand. I'll have them in a minute. I'm almost finished then you and me can mark out the field, Harry. I've brought a tape measure and some string and a few wooden pegs. It shouldn't take us long.'

Harry checked his watch.

'What time do you finish?'

'Half four. But my boss said to work until the job's done.'

'Overtime?'

'No. I've volunteered to do it.'

'You'll be upsetting the union.'

'I don't think so. They moan a lot but they're a good bunch really. Apart from the odd one or two. Nearly everybody offered to volunteer once they knew it was for Woodland House.'

They left Bill to finish the grass cutting and walked back to the children's play area, Harry pushing the line marking machine like a new parent with a pram, and Brian at his side carrying the heavy bag of powder. Brian put his sunglasses on and scanned the newly mown grass.

'It's going to look fabulous when it's all done and all marked out and the goal posts are up.'

'And my super-duper new corner flags are in place.'

'Yes. They look great. I've got butterflies already. It's like being a young man again getting ready to play in my first cup final.'

As Harry unloaded the wheelbarrow, a white van pulled into the car park. The driver jumped out and looked around the park and then waved at Brian and Harry. She was wearing a red and black tracksuit and a black baseball cap.

'She looks like that coach from that Masons FC team you played the other week.'

Harry shielded his eyes from the sun.

'It is. It's Janice. She'll have brought the goal posts and nets from Sheffield for us.'

Harry teamed up with Bill to mark out the pitch, and Brian helped Janice unload the aluminium posts and the bag of nets. They carried the lightweight posts down the gravel path to the children's play area, and Janice showed Brian how to assemble them and attach the nets. As they were carrying the first of the completed goal posts across the newly mown grass to where Bill and Harry were marking out the goal lines, a flat-bed truck arrived in the car park. Brian recognised the cargo straightaway. It was a blue and white portable toilet. He had experienced the pleasure of using one hundreds of times over the years while working on various building sites, where the telephone kiosk-like structure was affectionately known as the turdis.

The driver skilfully hoisted the unit off the back of the truck and set it down at the side of the flower bed. The driver joked he had picked the blue loo specially to go with the red, blue, and white begonias. As soon as the truck pulled away, people began to walk around the portable toilet, eyeing it with suspicion as though it had landed from another planet.

Around one o'clock, another white van pulled into the carpark and Harry and Brian helped the driver unload a dozen folding tables and set them up near the children's play area overlooking the pitch. Over the next fifteen minutes, more small vans and hatchbacks pulled into the carpark. People in hats, sunglasses, shorts, T-shirts and flip-flops opened boots and side doors, and dragged out kettles and urns, coffee making machines, cardboard boxes full of sandwiches, pop and cakes, jars of honey, boiled sweets and chocolates, and carried them across the grass to the tables.

The sellers, most of them from the shops on Clayton high street knew what they were doing. Harry was happy to let them get on with it and he sat down on the grass with Brian in the shade of a tree at the side of the flower bed and watched the action. A boy in a straw hat at least three sizes too big for his head, struggling to look over the top of the cardboard box he was carrying, stumbled on his way to a table. The box fell to the floor and paper cups spilt out onto the grass. A woman wearing faded denim dungarees came out from behind her stall and helped the boy gather the cups up and together they carried the box over to his table. A man and a woman with a dog were the first to buy a coffee and a cake from one of the stalls, and within minutes there was a queue at every table. More people came into the park.

At half past two a minibus arrived, and the Clayton colliery band, smartly dressed in white shirts and red trousers with a black stripe down the side, stepped out and unloaded their instruments and music stands. The people queuing outside the stalls smiled and parted to let them through and the band joked with them and smiled back. The conductor rigged up his music stand in the bandstand, already swept out and set up with chairs, and the band members settled into their new surroundings.

People started to congregate around the bandstand. Some had brought insulated picnic bags and parasols and folding camping chairs. Others were happy to sit on tartan blankets, or directly on the dry grass, and all of them claimed a little piece of the park for themselves.

'I love a good brass band,' Harry said. 'We're lucky we've still got our colliery band here in Clayton. As soon as I hear them strike up I'm back at the pit.'

'My dad worked at Nordem Main before it shut.'

'I worked there myself for a year. I knew your dad. He was a good worker. I was at Clayton pit for five years then I ended up wagon driving. I came into mining at the back end but mining's in my blood.'

'Do you miss it, being a miner?'

'Sometimes I do. It was good money and there were some good blokes there.' Harry stood up and stared at the blue, cloudless sky. 'But in many ways this is as good a job as I've ever had: giving my time and what few skills I have for a worthy cause.'

'All voluntary? I take my hat off to you, Harry.'

'I do get a free lunch, and the jam roly-poly is out of this world.'

The band began to tune up, the crowd went quiet and children were instructed in vain to sit still. The conductor raised his baton, the players sat up, and he asked them if they were ready. And they were off. The sudden bright sound burst out of the bandstand, filling the park, and heads nodded in tune and little children danced on the spot to their own music.

"Florentiner March," Harry said. 'A good tune to march to.'

'It certainly gets you going. It's like a magnet. Look at all those folk coming into the park with their pushchairs and dogs and the little kids on their bikes. It's like looking at a Lowry painting only everybody looks happy.'

'It's good to see so many parents and youngsters out enjoying the sunshine instead of being stuck inside on their mobiles and computers.'

'Isn't it just.'

Brian lifted up his sunglasses and put them down again.

'I keep looking for a mountain bike. I'm expecting Duggan to show up any minute. He'll be out there somewhere, spying. He'll know exactly what's going on, and he'll not be happy that Jean's managed to pull all this together.'

'He seems like the kind of bloke who always wants to be in charge.'

'You've got him.'

'We had plenty of those at the pit.'

'Have you noticed how nobody's walking on the pitch now that it's been marked out? You'd think there was an electric fence around it. Hello. I might have spoken too soon. Those young lads on their bikes behind the nets look as though they're daring each other to be the first to ride onto the field.'

'I wouldn't worry about them, Brian. It's only young cheeky Ryan and his mates. Jean's given them a job to do. She's told them to make sure nobody messes about with the nets or drops any litter on the field before kick-off. And to make sure no dogs go anywhere near the playing surface.'

'She's got more faith in young people than I have.'

'She knows their mothers.'

Brian smiled to himself. Another win for Jean. He was thinking a lot about Jean lately. It was to do with football and coaching and the way she handled people. It was to do with the caring way she and her team looked after his dad and the other residents. And it was to do with something else; Christmas day and no trimmings up. Only a photograph of Susan for company. Jean walking into his front room, smiling. Brian not knowing where to look.

The image drifted away, replaced by the kids playing on the swings and the slide and the carousel. The people queueing at the busy food stalls. The growing audience in front of the bandstand. The youths on cycles patrolling the untouchable pitch. The bandstand clock stuck on five to twelve, oblivious to everything around it. Brian's heart missed a beat.

'It's a fair crowd already, Harry. I'm getting nervous. It'll be like entering an arena tonight when the two teams walk out onto the pitch.'

'I'm getting nervous for Jean and the lasses.'

'Right. Do you want me for anything else? I need to be getting home for a bite to eat and then I've got to pick our Jeff up.'

'No, I think that's it. I'll just make sure cheeky Ryan and his mates are happy with everything and then I'll get back up to Woodland House. I've a window to fix.' Harry looked at his watch. 'Not long to go now.'

On his way to the car park, Brian got a call from Malc.

'Col's just phoned me. He said that ex-pro ref mate of Duggan's, him that's supposed to be reffing the match tonight, he says we're not covered by the rules of the FA and we'll have to cancel the match.'

'What's he on about, cancel the match?'

'Something to do with men not being allowed to play against women in an official game of football.'

'Bollocks. It's only a friendly.'

'That's what I said. But Col said Duggan's registered the men's team with the FA. That means any game they play falls within their laws.'

'Leave it with me, Malc. I'll find out what the hell Duggan's playing at. Don't say anything to anybody. If anybody asks, the game's going ahead.'

'It might be too late. Duggan's already told the players it's off.'

Brian rammed his phone into his back pocket and kicked an empty coke can deep into the hedge bottom.

'I'll swing for that bastard.'

On his way to the car park he was stopped by a man carrying a camera on his shoulder and a boom microphone in his hand.

'Excuse me,' the cameraman said. 'Is this where the football match between Carers United and the New Acorn is taking place this evening?'

Brian checked to see if there were any red lights lit up on the man's camera and microphone. The guy looked friendly and trustworthy but Brian had been wary of reporters ever since his dad told him about the press coverage of the miners' strike.

'That's right. Six o'clock kick-off.'

'I'm looking for Jean, the senior care worker at Woodland House care home. Do you happen to know where the home is?'

'Your best bet is to talk to that gentleman down there under that tree with the wheelbarrow. He's in charge.'

Brian rang Duggan from his van. His hands were sweating, a cold kind of sweat.

'What's all this about the FA and you cancelling the match tonight?'

'That's correct. It's not my decision; it's FA rules. A men's team is not allowed to play against a women's team in any officially organised match.'

'Why didn't you tell me you were registering the New Acorn with the FA? I could have told Jean. She's spent hours organising tonight's game.'

'I assumed she'd looked into it. She seems to have all the answers.'

Brian ended the call while Duggan was still talking. He rang Malc.

'Can you use that fancy phone of yours and find out who's in charge of the FA in this area. I think it comes under Sheffield. It would have to be a bloody Saturday afternoon.'

While Brian was waiting in his van, his phone buzzed with texts from the New Acorn players asking if the match was on or off. He read the short messages over and over again. What to do? It'll be a chuffing hoax, he said out loud to himself. Duggan's making it up. He's a bad loser. Ignore him. Ring round everybody and play the match as planned. Even if Duggan's telling the truth, the FA would never find out. And if they did it'd be too late for them to do anything about it. Unless somebody got badly injured or there was serious crowd trouble. It'd be in all the papers. Shit. Okay then. Field two mixed teams and call them...I don't know...Carers 1 against Carers 2, anything. The FA can't stop us doing that. Yes, but the crowd are expecting to see a team of young women carers take on a team of middle-aged blokes who used to be good. That's the whole point. That's the battle. That's where the money will come from for the care home. The crowd will not be happy with anything less. Bloody hell. What will Jean say?

His phone rang. It was Malc. He'd gone into the FA's website and found a telephone number. He'd tried it five times but it kept going to the answer machine. He'd made a note of their email address if that was any good.

'It's too late for that, Malc. Give me the phone number. I'll keep trying. In the meantime, if anybody rings you, the match is still on.'

'Keep calm, Brian. We'll think of something.'

Jean was doing her books at Woodland House when Brian stopped at the side of her desk. He took his phone away from his ear and turned it off, the endless, tuneless engaged tone still playing in his head. Jean smiled at him and rubbed her hands.

'Are you getting as nervous as me, Brian? There's a wonderful atmosphere here in the home. Everybody's talking about the game.'

'I was nicely nervous until half an hour ago. Now I'm panicking.'

Brian told Jean about Duggan and the FA.

'I can't get hold of anybody at the FA. They've all gone home. Chuffing Duggan.'

'Don't panic.'

Jean closed her file and scrolled through the contacts on her mobile. She tapped the screen, stood up, nodded to Brian to take a seat and went over to the dining room window.

'Good afternoon, Charles. Nothing to worry about. Your mother's fine. She's just had her tea and now she's having a nap. I need a big favour. Do you still keep in contact with your old work colleagues at the FA...?'

When Brian got back in his van, he rang Duggan and offered him the chance to ring round the men's team and tell them the match was back on. Otherwise he would ring them and explain the mix-up. The phone went quiet.

Brian pipped his horn and waited outside Jeff's house. There was no point in turning the engine off. On some occasions he didn't even get as far as sounding the horn; the front door would open as soon as the van entered the cul-de-sac. His brother must be on high alert, spying from behind the curtains. Or maybe he'd set up a trip wire. What excuse had he given to June this time? Would he come out of the house with his football gear in a brown paper bag? What a performance. Why didn't he have the guts to tell June about their dad having dementia?

167

Brian pipped his horn a second time. Where the hell is he? He switched off the engine. After five minutes of waiting he got out of the van and knocked on the front door. He stood back expecting Jeff to dash out, breathless and say let's go. The door did open. It was June.

'You'd better come in.'

Jeff was sitting on the couch in the living room. His head was down and he was blowing his nose. June took the tissue off him and pulled a fresh one out of the box on the coffee table. Brian sat on the edge of the armchair opposite and reached out to his brother, a few inches short of touching him.

'What's the matter, Jeff?'

June joined Jeff on the couch and put her arm around his shoulders and he sobbed gently. Tears dripped off his chin onto the front of his shirt darkening the cotton.

'Jeff's just told me about your dad.'

Brian felt relieved and he almost said thank God, but there was sadness and anger in the air and he checked himself.

'Has he.'

'I told June I hadn't even been to see him at the care home because I was too frightened it might upset her.'

'You're too right it might upset me. Just because your dad's in a home doesn't mean I can forgive him for all these years of torment he's put you and me through.' June glared at Brian. 'And you made it worse. Taking your dad's side. And Susan as well. That really hurt.'

'Don't go down that path, June. Our Brian and Susan never knew what came between us and my dad. I know that from my mother. You can't blame them.'

Brian was about to plead ignorance but the speed at which June stood up forced him to sit back in his chair.

She leaned over the coffee table and jabbed her finger at him, each jab reinforcing her angry words. Jab, shout, jab, shout.

'You never tried to understand, did you? You never once came round to see how we felt. You treated me and Jeff like lepers. Like we were dirt. You never cared about what we were going through. You're only interested now because your dad's in a home and you're feeling guilty. You're not thinking about me and Jeff. You don't care. You never have. Just like your dad.'

'Hang on, June. Me and Susan tried to find out what had gone off but you both clammed up on us. We'd no idea what had gone off.'

Jeff had stopped crying now and he put his hand on June's arm and she sank back onto the couch with her head down.

'Nobody knows what I went through. Sixteen and still at school. And suddenly there I am. Pregnant. Hiding the bump from my mother and father. God, if my mother had found out...' June shook her head and breathed in. 'Moving into a downtrodden flat with my boyfriend, hardly a penny between us. Then nine months later, a disabled baby to look after and a boyfriend who couldn't leave me fast enough. I couldn't cope. How could anybody cope in that situation?'

Brian slowly leaned forward again, this time covering his mouth with his hands as though praying.

'I wanted the best for the baby,' June said. 'He needed a family who could raise him; a family who could give him all the medical care and attention that I could never give him. I wanted him to have a life full of opportunities and love. That's not giving up the baby, is it?'

Jeff put his arms around his wife.

'You know you did the right thing, June. It was a loving and courageous thing to do. You were protecting the baby.'

'I tried my best.'

'When me and June decided to get married, my mother was all happy and soppy, talking about grandchildren as though we were going to have the patter of tiny feet running around the place in no time.'

'We thought we were doing the right thing, telling your mother and dad about what had happened to me at school. About my baby.'

'We told them there was a risk of June having another disabled baby if she got pregnant again.'

'Your mother started crying for us. She understood. But not your dad. He just asked what had happened to the baby so I told him.'

'He went off his head. He told June never to set foot in his house again. My mother tried to reason with him but his mind was made up. You know what he's like. I asked him what would happen if we decided to have children. Would they be welcome in his home? He said my grandchildren would be welcome and I would be welcome. But not June.'

'He didn't even say my name. He just said not her.'

'I felt sick. Sick that my own flesh and blood could do something so cruel, not just to me and June but to my mother as well. I said if June's not welcome, then none of us are welcome.'

June's eyes were red and dry.

'Your dad looked Jeff straight in the eye and said so be it.'

Brian stood up and put his arms around them both.

'Why didn't you tell me and Susan? We knew something major must have gone off for you all to fall out like you did but we'd no idea what had happened. My mother wouldn't tell us and my dad refused to talk about it. And we didn't like to probe. Then it got while we daren't even talk about it.

'I can't imagine how you must have felt making that decision about your baby, all on your own, June, and so young. I nearly cracked up when I had to make the decision to put my dad into a care home. I was on my own like you. There was nobody to talk it through with. I knew I couldn't ask you, Jeff. I just wish I'd been brave enough to have had it out with you. We might have sorted things out sooner. Got everything out in the open. The whole episode of putting my dad into care hit me hard. It was a lonely period in my life. I was desperate for someone to help me out. At the time I resented you for not being there to share the load. Now I feel bad. Really bad.'

The grandfather clock in the hallway struck five o'clock and as the chimes rang out Brian slowly sat back down. June dabbed her eyes and cheekbones.

'I bet I look a right mess.'

Jeff blew his nose.

'Not as bad as me.'

'You both look a right mess,' Brian said, and he reached over and pulled a tissue out of the box on the table. 'You'll have me going next.'

'I never wanted Jeff to suffer. He was already suffering enough.'

Jeff held June's hand.

'I wasn't suffering anywhere near as much as you were suffering, love.'

'I didn't realise how much you missed not seeing your dad. I should have known. Then when you told me he was in a home...'

Brian stood up and took his van keys out of his pocket.

'Jeff. If you don't want to come with me, that's fine. I'll manage.'

'It's okay,' June said. 'No need for any more pretence. Jeff's told me you're playing football against a team of women from your dad's care home.'

'I think I'll sit this one out, Brian. I think me and June could do with a glass of wine on our own tonight and a chance to recover.'

'I've recovered already,' June said. 'I feel better now than I have done for years. Where are you playing?'

Brian let his brother answer.

'Woodland Park in Clayton village. Six o'clock kick off.'

'Give me five minutes to put my mascara on and I'll join you. It's been ages since you took me to a football match.'

'We're all meeting up for a barbecue back at my house after the match, if you fancy it. There'll be plenty to eat and drink.'

June looked at Jeff and smiled.

'That'll be great.'

18

Jean tucked her clipboard under her arm and clapped her hands.

'Are we ready then, girls?'

'We are,' Kalina said. 'Come on. This is our day.'

The tall goalkeeper stood up and bounced the new white football on the tiled floor, the low thud filling the laundry room at Woodland House like a bass drum.

Gloria, sleeves rolled up, tattoo on display, was the next to stand up and she made her way round her team mates one by one shaking their shoulders, telling them how good they were, staring into their eyes, her face so close to theirs her words made them blink. The rest of the team got to their feet and the clatter of rubber studs added background percussion to the boom, boom of Kalina's bouncing ball.

Jean led them out as a unit, note book and clipboard in hand, chest out. In the late afternoon sunshine, stepping out of the laundry room, kitted out in their brand new purple shirts, black shorts and purple socks with white double stripes, the team looked as though it had just been washed, dried and ironed. They left Woodland House car park and walked down the lane in buddy pairs towards the high street with Harry and his heavy pack of water bottles and trainer's bag a few yards behind. The figure standing in the dark entrance to the boxing club in the former Methodist Chapel, straightened up as Jean and her team approached. It was Pete. As soon as Jean saw him, he slipped back into the gym no doubt to tell Tommy Duggan that the women were up for it.

There was hardly anyone on the high street and the road was quiet enough to cross without using the zebra crossing. Two men outside the Miners Arms pub, casually smoking their cigarettes as though they owned the establishment, pints balanced and glinting on the sunny window sill, wolf whistled at the women as they walked by.

'Come on the lasses. Hammer the boys.'

'We'll do our best,' Jean said.

The team turned into the car park and got their first glimpse of the park. Jean slowed and the team closed up behind. You couldn't see the grass around the bandstand and the food stalls for people in T-shirts, shorts and sun hats, sitting, standing and strolling between the attractions. In the play area, the swings were occupied by kids too old to be on them, young children queued for the slides, and a lad in a baseball cap jumped off the overcrowded carousel and tried to get back on again.

'What a welcome, girls,' Jean said. 'Let's do them proud.'

The team set off along the gravel path in formation and the view of the playing area opened up. Their former rough training area had been transformed into a close-mown, immaculately marked out seven-a-side football pitch. Already at twenty to six, women and girls lined one touch line. Down the opposite touch line a few men and boys stood in ones and twos. Cheeky Ryan and his mates had thrown their bikes down behind one of the nets and were sitting cross legged on the grass keeping an eye on the crowd. As Jean led her team towards the football pitch the Carers United supporters cheered and clapped and the band started playing 'The William Tell

Overture'. Kalina kicked her ball towards the goal nearest the flower bed and the team ran onto the pitch, fanning out, jumping high, running on the spot then zig-zagging away in body-swerving dashes.

Opposite the half way line, supporters moved out of the way to make space for the Carers United dugout. Jean put her notebook and clip board on top of the first aid box and Harry put down his trainer's bag and heavy water bottles.

'Well, Harry,' Jean said. 'We've won the battle for support.'

'We certainly have. Where have all these women and girls come from? If the pitch was a see-saw those blokes and young lads over there on the other side would be watching the game ten foot up in the air.'

Janice, the coach from Masons FC, now dressed in her black referee's assistant's outfit, had been standing among the line of women and girls and she came over and joined Jean and Harry.

'What a great turn out. We never get crowds as big as this back in Sheffield. Good luck.'

It was ten minutes to kick off, and Jean once again crosschecked her training notes with the notes Harry had made on his spying mission to Aspinal Rec's training ground.

'Stuart's the one to watch,' Harry said. 'He's their best finisher.'

'Kalina knows what to expect. He'll shoot from any angle. Brian says Alan holds their defence together. We need to drag him wide.'

Their discussion on tactics was interrupted by good-natured booing from the women supporters. The referee in his all black outfit was walking towards the pitch, sharing something funny with Duggan and Pete.

Behind them in a straggle came the New Acorn side in their all white strip, a few players in shirts too tight to tuck in over their bellies. And Brian was at the back.

Brian waved to Jean, nothing too obvious, and she waved back. What he would give now to be standing alongside her as assistant coach, supporting Carers United instead of playing against them.

He jogged towards the goal opposite the Carers United end and Col, his homemade liniment smelling of mothballs and vinegar, came past with an exaggerated knee lift. He was well padded up, one bandage short of a mummy. The rest of the men's team were in no hurry to join Brian and Col. They were too busy laughing at Steve and his bright orange building site ear defenders, pretending to be listening to his personal stereo, in a different world, like a top professional player getting off the team coach.

Phil had his own ball and he jogged past Brian to the corner flag a few yards from a scattering of men and boy supporters. He began a session of keep-up; left foot, right foot, left knee, right knee. Twelve times. Superb. Going well. Oops, dropped it. Roll it onto the right foot, start again as though planned. Another sixteen. Phil tried to conclude his display by spreading his arms and trapping the ball behind his neck. But it rolled down his back and for a few seconds he couldn't work out where it had gone. His head had a swagger to it and he tried to look as though he had meant to end the little virtuoso performance that way. But the young lads weren't fooled and they laughed at him and one shouted, 'Throw him a fish'.

As Brian predicted, most of the women supporters had their eyes on one player. Someone in the crowd wolf whistled as Stuart left his cigarettes and lighter with his girlfriend, Aami and kissed her on the cheek before strolling onto the pitch, apparently unaware of the effect he was having on the women. Cool or what.

While the Carers United team were stretching and sprinting and passing the ball to each other, the New Acorn players were taking turns to shoot at goal, whooping and roaring at their own efforts. Brian joined in, twenty one again. Jeff was on form, saving nine out of ten shots, each save applauded by a smiling June on the touch line. When he tipped a hard strike from Brian over the bar he went down on one knee and grabbed the lower half of his back. Malc put his mobile in his tracksuit pocket, picked up his trainer's bag and jogged over to the goal area. Jeff was okay, just a muscle strain, and after a rub and a blast of freeze spray he went back between the posts. Malc stayed on the field, pretending to organise the contents of his trainer's bag.

'Brian. Here.'

'What's up?'

'I've just been looking on the internet. That referee Duggan's brought with him. His name's Billy Wilkinson. He was banned from refereeing by the FA ten years ago.'

'Banned? For what?'

'Taking bribes.'

'Fucking Duggan. Don't say anything to anybody. Let's see what happens.'

Malc picked up his trainer's bag, put his hand on Brian's shoulder and winked.

'Jean's been looking at you ever since we ran onto the field. Nice one. It's about time. I was going to set you up on a dating app.'

Ten minutes before kick-off a mini bus arrived in the car park. Brian's dad along with Mary and a few other residents were helped into wheelchairs by care workers and pushed all the way through the park to a safe place near the touch line. There was a tall, suntanned man with them, mid-thirties, carrying a black and white holdall. That must be Jon Hunt, the owner of the three care homes. The man took a foot high silver cup out of the holdall and placed it on a table at the side of the wheelchairs.

'Look over there, Col,' Brian said.

Col rubbed his hands, did a few extra high knee lifts, and headed in a few imaginary crosses.

'I feel another trophy coming my way, Brian.'

The cameraman Brian had met earlier was crouching in front of the table taking shots of Jon Hunt and the trophy from different angles. He took a sweeping shot of the crowd and the park and finished with a close up of the care workers looking after his dad and Mary and the other residents in the wheelchairs.

Brian's dad was staring across the field. He had his dad's football boots in his lap. Brian shouted to Jeff and they jogged over. Mary saw them first.

'What a beautiful evening for a sports day.'

'It is, Mary,' Brian said. 'Beautiful. Hello, Dad. Wish me and our Jeff good luck.'

'Good luck boys. Who's in goal?'

'I am, Dad.'

'Keep a clean sheet, Jeff; I'm coming on in the second half.'

Jeff turned his head and covered his eyes. Brian rubbed his brother's back and smiled at Mary. Their dad tried to remove his woollen gloves, pulling at the finger ends, working out how to take them off.

'You can borrow my goalkeeping gloves,' he said. 'You'll catch the ball better. They've never let me down.'

One of the carers gently pushed the gloves back on and told him he needed to keep his hands warm if he was going on in the second half.

Two minutes to kick off and the 'Liberty Bell,' one of Jean's favourite brass band tunes, came to a perfectly timed ending. The referee and his two assistants, Janice and Pete, walked to the centre spot and signalled they were ready. Jean shouted her final words of encouragement to her team; it was up to them now.

She had calculated the men, especially Steve and Brian, being much slower than the women, would stay in their own half and leave a lone striker up front. They would back off and resist making a tackle which, if lost, would leave their defence exposed. This ploy was designed to invite the fitter, younger women to attack and then if the women lost possession, the men would counter attack and get the ball up to Stuart, the lone striker as fast as they could.

She was right. Early in the game, despite the intricate, entertaining runs from Aisha and Anne, the Carers United attack found it hard to penetrate the wall put up by the New Acorn defence. On the rare occasion when an attacker managed to get past the midfield of Brian, Steve and Col, a majestic Alan would sweep them away with a well-timed interception. Helen and Sheila's powerful shooting remained long range and caused Jeff few problems. Jean flicked through her notes, and Harry gave his opinion.

Eight minutes into the game, Gloria, the sole defender on guard against a New Acorn counter attack, made a crunching tackle on Col in midfield. The ball broke free and Stuart nicked it and ran towards goal. Anne and

Mahsa, no slouches, were too far up front to get back and it was left to a scrambling Gloria to try and catch him. Kalina came out of her goal and spread her arms and legs to cut down the angle, but Stuart kept his cool and struck the ball low into the corner of the net. The crowd of women moaned and the scattering of men and boys clapped and cheered.

1-0 to the New Acorn.

The same thing happened five minutes later.

2-0 to the New Acorn.

Stuart was on a hat-trick. Jean changed tactics and pulled Helen back to help Gloria even though that meant the forwards lost their most powerful ball striker. Jean shouted to Aisha and called her over.

'Play down the lines, drag the defenders wide.'

Jean calculated the New Acorn players wouldn't be able to resist moving up into the space left in midfield, despite Duggan's loud warnings from the line opposite. It worked. Aisha ran through the defence and hit an unstoppable shot into the back of the net before Alan could close her down. The crowd of women and girls cheered and even a few men clapped. Alan nodded to Aisha as she ran past to celebrate with the rest of the team and told her it was a good goal.

2-1 to the New Acorn.

At half time, the band played Abba's 'I Believe in Angels'. Nathan and Chloe with little Summer bouncing and laughing in her mother's arms, set off round the touch lines shaking a red bucket with a sticker on the side saying 'Care for Carers'.

Jean gathered her team in a semi-circle and told them to sit down and rest. Gloria and Helen shook their tight hamstring muscles and Harry handed out the water bottles.

'Come on, girls,' Jean said, making eye contact with each player. 'Victory is within our grasp. The men are tiring fast. All we have to do is play like we did in the last ten minutes of the first half, be patient, and the game is there for the taking.'

'You didn't tell us they were that fit and fast, Tommy,' Stuart said, and he stubbed out his half time cigarette against his boot.

All the players were lying flat out on the grass except Jeff. He was stretching his sides and jumping on the spot, the back muscle strain healed.

'Come on, lads,' he said. 'Let's look as though we want to win this game.'

'Win it?' Steve said. 'We'll be lucky to finish it.'

Col pushed his white socks down and tested the tape holding his shin pads in place.

'It's a good job I've got my pads on. That chunky lass with the ginger hair and the tattoos at the back, she nearly took my legs off.'

Col's legs were thin and white, and his rolled down socks looked like two grommets around his ankles.

'That's Gloria,' Brian said. 'She's a tough cookie.'

Over on the other side of the pitch, the Carers United team were back on their feet, ready for the start of the second half. Duggan put his hands in his pockets.

'You look like a shower of shit. Stop fannying around. Treat these women like blokes and get stuck in.'

The referee blew for the start of the second half and within five minutes, Jean's prediction proved to be right; the men's team tired quickly. Aisha and Sylvia were finding more space now and that gave the women renewed energy and confidence. Kalina rolled the ball out to Gloria on the edge of the penalty area. When she tried to pass it to Mahsa, Phil read the move and got a foot to the ball. Gloria pounced and recovered the ball cleanly to applause from Jean and Harry, but Phil fell to the floor and cried out in pain. The referee blew for a penalty and the crowd of women booed.

Jean shook her head.

'If that's a penalty, I'm Lady Godiva.'

Phil scored from the spot and, jabbing his chest and kissing his shirt ran past the booing supporters.

3-1 to the New Acorn.

Jean shouted to her players to push forward and within two minutes a one-two between Mahsa and Anne made Steve look like a bystander and took Anne to the goal line. Her low cross to the near post found Helen and she deflected the ball into the net for Carers United's second goal.

3-2 to the New Acorn. Five minutes to go.

All the New Acorn players with the exception of Alan were reduced to jogging, coughing, and walking and when beaten to the ball, resorted to pulling the women's shirts and shoulder charging. Jean noticed Jeff was good in the air but not so good on the ground. She passed a message to Aisha telling her not to be afraid to shoot low and hard whenever she felt she was in range. The plan worked and two minutes later Aisha scored.

3-3. One minute to go.

The crowd cheered and clapped and the noise enticed the few remaining visitors away from the food stalls and brought them to the pitch side.

Aisha received the ball from Gloria in her own half on the touch line where the women supporters were standing and cheering. Brian was the closest New Acorn player to her. Aisha knew from Jean's coaching that Brian was slow on the turn. He would know how fast she was. That's why he held off hoping she would pass the ball infield. Aisha had other ideas. She ran straight at him causing him to back pedal. She feigned to go left then right. It was so clever, Jean and Harry body swerved with her. Brian would have to make a tackle or be left stranded. He lunged forward but Aisha tapped the ball through his legs and by the time he turned to see what had happened, she was ten yards down the line. Some wag on the touch line shouted 'Nutmeg' and the crowd roared. A few supporters stepped onto the pitch to try and track Aisha's run. Pete, flag in hand, had to shout for them to stand back so he could see down the line. Aisha cut inside and before Alan could close her down, shot low and hard. The ball glanced off the far post into the net. Jeff never moved. The crowd cheered and as Aisha was being mobbed by her team mates the referee blew his whistle.

'No goal. The ball was out of play.'

The crowd booed. Gloria led the team protest and somehow she and Anne managed not to swear at the referee. Jean stepped a yard onto the field and told the referee he had made a mistake.

'Ask the linesman,' she said. 'He was closer than you. He didn't flag. It never went out. Did it Pete?'

Duggan strode ten yards onto the field from the other touch line and shouted loud enough for Jean and the Carers United team to hear.

'The ball was miles out. You could see from here. Tell the ref, Pete. It was out.'

Pete froze, flag drooping down by his side. The crowd went quiet and everyone waited for his reaction.

Jean whispered to Harry.

'What's Brian up to?'

Brian was twenty yards away from Jean, ten yards from Pete. He started walking slowly towards Pete, talking quietly to him all the time. It was the only sound and movement on the pitch.

'Pete. We all know it was in. Don't let Tommy bully you into cheating. For once in your life, stand up to him. Do it for the game, Pete. Do it.'

Pete put his head down and after a few seconds walked across to the referee to the sound of murmuring from the crowd. There was a fifteen second consultation. The referee pointed towards the centre circle and the crowd went wild.

4-3 to Carers United. Seconds to go.

Four minutes later and the referee still hadn't blown the final whistle. People were looking at their watches and mobile phones. Harry told Jean there was something fishy going on.

'I think this ref's set his watch by that bandstand clock. We'll be here till five to bloody midnight.'

They played another full two minutes and the score remained the same. The referee made a big point of looking at his watch and then turned his back on Duggan and blew his whistle. The game was over.

The Carers United players hugged each other and Jean and Harry jogged over to them and they were hugged. The women shook hands with the men and Steve suggested they swap shirts. Gloria said she would gladly swap shirts with Stuart.

Jean met Duggan on the half way line and held out her hand.

'Hard luck. It was a good game.'

'If you say so.'

'See you back at Brian's for the barbecue?'

'Maybe.'

The two teams stayed apart and waited on the field for the trophy to be presented, the New Acorn players sitting on the grass, muttering, and the Carers United players in a huddle, laughing and touching. Brian's dad was asleep in his wheelchair near the touch line, still clutching his dad's old football boots.

'Leave him in peace, Jeff,' Brian said. 'The old lad's worn out.'

'It was all those magnificent saves he made in the second half.'

Mary was helped out of her wheelchair by a care worker and, once confident and able to stand unaided, was invited to present the trophy to the winning team. She shook hands with each player, touching them on their cheek, telling them they were some of the most talented schoolgirls she had ever had the privilege of teaching. Gloria held the trophy in the air and everyone clapped including the New Acorn players and a reluctant Duggan.

Jon Hunt thanked the crowd for turning out in their hundreds, and for digging deep into their pockets in support of the village and Woodland House care home. He thanked all those who had made the day such a wonderful success. And last but by no means least he gave a special thanks to Jean and the care home staff, not forgetting Harry the evergreen volunteer handyman, for putting on such an entertaining spectacle. This got the loudest cheer and the longest applause. He promised the crowd the event would be covered in next month's Care Home magazine and he wouldn't be at all surprised to see it in Friday's Brodworth Chronicle.

The trophy table was folded away and the crowd began to leave the park. Brian told Jeff and June he wanted to stay behind for a few minutes and take in the atmosphere.

'I'll catch up with you in a bit.'

The players followed his dad, Mary and the other residents being pushed along the gravel path towards the car park. All the way there, the two sides stayed separate: a block of purple leading a block of white. Jean wasn't with them. She was collecting the corner flags with Harry.

Brian sat on the wall of the flower bed, watching the crowd thin out and the council workers in their orange jackets pick up the litter. He recalled the events of the day, fixing them in his memory forever. His dad and Jeff had spoken for the first time in thirty years. Jeff and June were coming to the barbecue. And Jean. What a star. Carer. Coach. Possible girlfriend.

A thumping sound distracted him. The vacated bandstand had been taken over by cheeky Ryan and a gang of lads and lasses. One of them was bouncing a football off the ceiling, the sound amplified by the simple wooden dome structure.

Someone grabbed the ball and threw it out onto the grass which sparked a free for all with everyone tumbling out of the bandstand and sprinting after it. One of the young girls got to the ball first and she gave it a mighty hoof. It struck the bandstand clock and bounced up into the air. There was a race between a young lad and a young girl to catch the ball before it dropped out of the sky. As the pair's eyes tracked the ball's trajectory they ran into each other and fell to the ground in a tangle of limbs and laughter.

Harry was now half way up the gravel path with the corner flags under his arm. Jean was on her own on the halfway line fifty yards away. Was she too capturing the moment? Brian went over.

'Well done Jean on organising a great day's entertainment and making a great match of it.'

'And thanks to you for getting your team to take on the challenge. It was a tough game. Just what we needed.'

The two teams had reached the car park now. Jon Hunt was in the middle of both sets of players, shaking their hands, and the cameraman was walking among them taking candid shots from various angles.

'Looking at them mixing together in the car park you'd think things had changed,' Brian said. 'But Steve will still be telling the same old jokes and holding the same old sexist and racist views. Phil will still only be interested in the great goals he scored when he was their age. Duggan will still be bullying everybody around him. Nothing will have changed.'

'But things have changed, Brian. Today, the women won. And they won because they cared.'

'I think my dad and the other residents who were there enjoyed the game as much as we did.'

'That's what it's all about. When I get into work tomorrow we'll be putting up the bunting and the balloons and getting out the party hats for everybody. And remembering Arthur. He would have loved to have been here for the game but sadly...'

'Arthur? He's not..?'

'This afternoon. Peacefully in his sleep.'

'That's so sad,' Brian said. 'I thought I hadn't seen him. He would have loved being out in the fresh air with Mary and my dad and the others. He'd have ripped that safety helmet off and thrown it in the air when that final whistle went.'

Brian checked the time on the bandstand clock out of habit and he had to look twice. It was twelve o'clock.

'Time's ticking by,' he said. 'We'd better be getting back. We've a barbecue to light.'

19

For the first time in five years, people, not starlings gathered on Brian's back lawn and he was happy. He even chuckled when the fat, dripping from the pork sausages and beef burgers he was turning on the cooking grate, spat at him. The hot smoke drifting up from the sizzling meat and onions burned his cheeks and made his eyes run and he didn't care.

Both teams had turned up for the after match barbecue and they were eating, drinking and chatting in the warm evening air. Jean had brought her CD player and speakers from her own home, together with some of her favourite soul dance music, and set it up on the patio wall. Already, less than an hour and a half after the final whistle had gone a party mood was building under the clear evening sky.

Gloria, Helen, Sheila and Mahsa were singing to each other with imaginary microphones. Kalina, Anne, and reserve keeper Sylvia were holding hands and dancing around the silver trophy, watched from a few yards away by Duggan and Pete, the two men looking worried in case they were asked to join in. Stuart had no such inhibitions; he was dancing loose-limbed in a corner of the garden with his girlfriend, Aami.

In front of the apple tree Susan and Brian had planted as a sapling when they first moved into the house, Jon Hunt and Harry were talking with the referee Billy Wilkinson. What were they discussing? Pruning a neglected fruit tree? Running a care home? Raising money for charity? Working with local communities? Volunteering? Bribery?

At the side of the greenhouse, Phil, his arms moving around like an orchestra conductor, was talking at Col no doubt about great goals and winning medals. And in front of the garden shed, Jeff and June were talking with Malc, heads down, no one taking over.

As Brian was tending the barbecue, Jean appeared at his side and pressed her hip against his thigh.

'Can I get you a lager, mister chef, all dressed up and looking good in your blue and white pinafore?'

'That would be great. I'm on fire here.'

'I've got some news for you.'

'Somebody's nicked all the beer.'

'No. Our Nathan's asked me to ask you if you'll give him a hand building that pigeon loft.'

'You're kidding me.'

'And you'll never guess what. Tommy Duggan's just told me his granddaughter wants to be a footballer when she grows up. He wants to know if he can bring her down to Woodland Park sometime to watch Carers United train.'

'I must be dreaming.'

Brian put his arm around Jean and kissed her and he didn't care who was watching.

Jean went over to the drinks table and as Brian placed a veggie burger on the cooking plate for himself someone shouted his name.

'Brian. Brian.' It was Col. He was pointing to the upstairs window. 'There's smoke coming out of your window.'

Brian spun round. He threw down the tongs and leapt up the steps to the patio decking and into the back room through the open patio doors. A few seconds later he ran back out.

'There's a chuffing fire in the hallway.'

He gripped the patio door. Grey smoke rolled along the ceiling towards him. He went back inside and tried again to get to the hallway but the smoke blocked his route. He came back out, white-faced, staring at the crowd on the lawn slowly closing in on him.

Harry pushed his way to the edge of the patio. The smoke coming out of the upstairs window was now almost as dark as the slates on the roof. Malc was on his mobile, eyes looking everywhere, one hand over his ear.

'Phone the fire brigade, Malc,' Harry said.

'I am doing.'

'Let me know as soon as they're on their way.'

'Will do.'

Harry put his hand on Brian's shoulder.

'Have you got a fire extinguisher, Brian?'

'No. No.'

'What about a hose pipe?'

'In my shed.'

Kalina and Jean jumped onto the patio and grabbed Brian's arms.

'Go and get it,' Kalina said. 'Try and put the fire out from here while you can still see inside.'

Brian hesitated. He'd heard the instructions but he could only stare into the back room and the smoke building up. Jeff freed himself from June's grip and jumped onto the decking.

'I'll get it, Brian. Is your shed open?'

'No. I mean yes.'

Jean ran down the patio steps.

'Helen, Anne, Mahsa. Fill some buckets and pans and anything else you can get your hands on and get into the kitchen fast. Throw as much water as you can into the hallway from that side.'

'There's some buckets in the garage,' Brian shouted as he ran the few yards to the outside stop tap under the kitchen window. 'The door's not locked. Yank it up, it's stiff.'

Kalina stood on the edge of the patio and scanned the faces of the crowd funnelling towards her on the lawn.

'Is everybody here? Is anyone upstairs?'

Brian shouted to his brother to be quick with the hose pipe and then turned to Kalina.

'Fucking hell. Please tell me nobody's upstairs.'

People looked to their side and behind. Gloria put her hand to her mouth.

'Where's Aisha?'

'She said she was going to the loo five minutes ago,' Sheila said.

Alan looked at the two cans of beer he was holding.

'Bloody hell. I think Steve might have gone to the toilet as well.'

There was a scream from upstairs and a cry for help. Brian put his arm across his mouth and nose and tried once again to enter the back room but got no nearer to the stairs.

'They're trapped, Kalina.'

Harry told Malc to phone for the ambulance as well as the fire service. Malc was talking quickly on the phone and he put his thumb up.

Jeff came running up the garden from the shed with the hose pipe under his arm. He uncoiled the pipe and dragged the gun end to the patio and Brian attached the open end to the stop tap. The pipe snagged against a corner of the low patio wall and kinked and Harry pulled it straight.

'Have you got a ladder and a torch, Brian?' Kalina said.

'My ladder's behind the garage. There's a torch under the kitchen sink. Go and get it, Jeff. I'll keep spraying.'

Kalina shouted to Jeff as he ran towards the kitchen door, 'And bring a tea towel.'

Harry asked for volunteers to fetch the ladder and immediately, Gloria, Col and Jean sprinted to the garage followed by Duggan, limping, trying his best to keep up.

The water pressure was good and Brian sprayed deep into the hallway without being blinded and choked by smoke. Every few seconds there was a flash as smoke turned to flame, and for an instant there was a glimpse of the staircase and the buckets of water being thrown from the other side by Helen, Anne and Mahsa. The white door and frame had turned yellow and the plastic was beginning to melt.

Jeff ran back with the torch and Kalina checked the strength of the beam. Brian, shirt pulled up to shield his face from the heat and smoke and the stench of burning plastic, had made a yard and was now spraying from the side of the sofa, still a long way from the staircase. Kalina tied the tea towel around her face.

'What are you doing?' Brian said.

'I'm going in through the upstairs window.'

'No you're not. I'll go in. I know my way around upstairs'

'I'm younger and fitter than you. You and Jeff concentrate on putting the fire out.'

'She's right, Brian,' Jeff said. 'Come on. Get some fresh air. My turn.'

June wiped Jeff's forehead with her sleeve and handed Brian some tissues.

'Be careful you two.'

People were getting in the way. June was beginning to panic. Harry told her to go to the end of the street and watch out for the fire service and ambulance. He calmly thanked everyone for keeping well back.

As Kalina tied the tea towel around her nose and mouth, Gloria, Col, Jean, with Duggan still trying to keep up, came running past Brian with the wooden ladder gripped lengthways like a battering ram. They set it up against the window and Jean and Col wedged the wooden feet into the turf and held it tight.

'I'll go in with you,' Duggan said. 'Get me a towel Pete.'

Kalina shook her head and through her face covering repeated what she had said to Brian.

'You can follow me up the ladder and wait at the top. Stay in contact. Keep calling out 'Kalina' and I'll keep calling out 'Tommy.''

The crowd moved in closer, their gaze switching between the upstairs window and the patio area. Brian held onto the patio door frame and shouted into the room.

'Are you okay, Jeff? Do you want me to take over?'

'I'm okay. I think we're getting on top of it. Keep the hose pipe clear.'

Kalina ran up the wooden ladder and was at the top before Duggan climbed two rungs. The old ladder flexed and creaked with each of Duggan's heavy footsteps. Kalina waited until his head was level with her feet.

'Are you ready?'

'Ready.'

She turned on the torch, climbed through the window and disappeared into the smoke. Duggan's shouts remained loud and clear but Kalina's became harder to hear as she went deeper into the smoke. The crowd went quiet, not even a whisper. Brian fed more hose pipe into the back room as Jeff made ground. The crowd heard Kalina call out to Aisha and Steve. A cry and a shout came straight back. The crowd cheered.

'She's found them, Jeff,' Brian said. 'Come on Kalina, lass. Get them out.'

Gloria climbed a few rungs to be closer to Duggan in case he needed support.

'Be careful with that ladder, Gloria,' Brian said. 'It's dodgy.'

Jean and Col dug their heels into the grass and gripped the base of the ladder even tighter.

Harry was the first to see Duggen stiffen. The tension rippled down the wooden rungs through Gloria to Jean to Col. Brian put his hands together and whispered, 'Please God.'

Something was happening behind the window. Or was it Duggan's reflection? People pointed and shouted. Then Duggan reached into the smoke and helped Aisha out onto the ladder. She dropped the blackened towel covering her face, and coughed and blinked. Brian joined the clapping and cheering and the noise didn't stop until she was safely off the ladder and into the arms of Jean and Gloria. Seconds later, another cheer went up as Steve climbed out through the window, blackened towel in hand, and breathed in the fresh evening air. As Duggan helped Steve down the ladder, Kalina climbed out and that got the loudest cheer and the biggest cry of relief.

Everyone pushed forward to be the first to hug Kalina and Aisha and grab Steve's hand. Jon Hunt and Harry brought three chairs out of the kitchen, and Sylvia filled three bottles with water to drink and pour into their sore eyes.

People were beginning to shift their focus back to Brian and the hosepipe when Jeff, Helen, Anne, and Mahsa came out through the patio doors.

'The fire's out,' they said together, and everyone clapped and shouted well done.

Brian hugged his four fellow fire fighters and went over to Kalina, Aisha and Steve, recovering in their chairs on the grassy area in front of the kitchen window.

'Kalina,' he said, shaking his head. 'You are one amazing woman. You deserve a medal for going into that smoke.'

She patted her chest and coughed.

'It was nothing. It had to be done.'

'And thank the Lord you two are alright.'

Steve, the colour coming back to his face, his breathing becoming less shallow, stared at Brian.

'I have never been so terrified in all my life. The heat up there. The smoke. I just panicked. I couldn't see a thing. I didn't know where the hell I was. I couldn't move. Jesus.'

'It was terrifying,' Aisha said between coughs. 'The staircase was full of smoke. It was so hot it felt like my hair was on fire. We couldn't see a thing in front of us, or behind us, or to the side of us. The air was getting hotter and hotter. We just held onto each other. Then we heard Kalina shouting out.'

'God, the heat and that dense smoke,' Steve said. 'I thought I was going to die.' He took a moment to breathe in and wipe his eyes. 'I'd gone upstairs to the toilet. I could smell smoke but I thought it was from the barbecue. Next thing somebody's braying on the door, screaming at me to get out.' He gently put his hand on Aisha's shoulder. 'Thank God you did, Aisha. I'd have still been trapped up there if you hadn't banged on the door and screamed. And thank God to you, Kalina for getting both of us out.'

196

'Yes, Kalina,' Aisha said. 'You saved our lives. You are a hero.'

Kalina rinsed her mouth and spat on the floor.

'You would have done the same for me.'

The three of them held hands. Brian got out of their way. For them, in that moment, there was no one else in the garden, and the crowd clapped for a long time.

It only took the fire service fifteen minutes to arrive and the ambulance came two minutes later. The paramedics attended to Kalina, Aisha and Steve and told them they were lucky to have suffered only singed hair and minor burns to the hands. There was no sign of shock. The face coverings had probably saved them from serious throat and lung damage.

The crew manager from the fire service confirmed they had checked inside the house and the fire was out.

'You and your guests have been very lucky,' she said to Brian. 'Did your smoke alarms go off?'

'No. They need new batteries.'

The only obvious damage was to the plastic door and frame, the paintwork on the skirting board, and the carpet in the hallway and the first few steps of the staircase. There was smoke damage in the hallway, the back room, up the staircase, and in the back bedroom. Luckily the bathroom door and the other two bedroom doors had been closed during the fire and so the damage was minimal. The water from the hose pipe and buckets had caused a little bit of damage but that was better than fire damage.

'Leave all the windows and doors open for at least a week,' the crew manager said.

'What do you think caused the fire?'

'It's hard to be sure. It doesn't look like an electrical fault or a gas leak. Was anyone smoking in the hallway? Or burning candles?'

'Not to my knowledge.'

'Have you upset anybody recently?'

Brian laughed.

'No more than usual.'

'I'll make arrangements for the Fire Investigation Officer to investigate.'

'Okay.'

When the ambulance and fire service had gone, the neighbour from across the road came over and joined Brian and Jean as they examined the damaged front door and the sodden hall carpet. The neighbour told Brian he had seen two lads on a scooter pull up outside Brian's house earlier that evening. The lad on the back delivered something through the letter box.

'I thought it was a new pizza delivery company,' the neighbour said. 'As if we haven't got enough of them in this village. They both had black and white crash helmets on, the ones with the big chin guards. They looked like they were off to do battle in an intergalactic war. They didn't hang around. I know they're on bonus but these two set off like a house on fire – sorry, Brian. I didn't mean to say that.'

The neighbour said to shout if there was anything he could do and he went back home.

'Two lads on a scooter?' Jean said to Brian as they walked hand in hand down the drive towards the back garden. 'Didn't you say you saw two lads on a scooter outside Aisha's friend's flat that day you were there?'

198

'I did. Black and white helmets and big chin guards. I'll bet the local authority have been round to the flats, asking questions.'

'Jon did say he'd spoken to them.'

'They'll have spooked the big chief – that big black guy in the BM. Spike must have told him who I was.'

'So they've sent those two lads round and set fire to your house? That's frightening.'

'I hope Spike's not involved. He's crazy but I don't think he'd have anything to do with setting fire to my house.' Brian pulled Jean close to him as they came round the corner of the house into the back garden. 'But if that's the price of caring for Aisha and her friend, so be it.'

The roof line on Brian's house stood out against the clear dark blue night sky. The full Moon was as yellow as the ball Kalina had gently lobbed to his dad that day at the home, when the old lad cried in fear, before sitting up and booting it into the ceiling light. Brian smiled and checked his watch.

'Half past nine. Is that all it is. Let's see if the barbecue's still got some life in it.'

Col had gone home to be with his wife. The remaining guests were quietly drinking and chatting in the light of the patio doors. They were quiet; too quiet. The outdoor party was coming to a premature end. Brian stepped onto the patio.

'There's plenty of beer and wine left. It's all got to go tonight; my fridge is waterlogged.'

Jean slotted a Tamla Motown disc into the CD player and turned the volume up. Players from Carers United and the New Acorn merged and danced around the silver trophy. Harry, Jon Hunt, Duggan and the referee, Billy Wilkinson split up and mingled with players from both sides. Brian grabbed Jean's hand, Jeff grabbed June's hand and they danced in front of the greenhouse. Martha Reeves and the Vandellas were on full volume.

'I wonder if my dad can hear us up at Woodland House,' Jeff said.

'No chance, bro. My dad'll be fast on after all the excitement he's had today.'

'We've all had a bit of excitement today,' June said, and she smiled at Jeff and that gave everyone else permission to smile.

'The lasses on night shift won't be able to hear us,' Jean said. 'They'll be too busy celebrating the football result.'

'Ah, you were lucky,' Brian said, smiling and winking at Jeff and June.

'Very lucky,' Jeff said. 'That last goal was never a goal.'

Jean spun on the spot to Dancing in the Street.

'Read next week's chronicle.'

BV - #0093 - 220725 - C0 - 198/129/15 - PB - 9781913625160 - Matt Lamination